The Last Laugh and Other Stories

Hugo Martínez-Serros

Arte Publico Press
Houston

Acknowledgements

This project is made possible through a grant from the National Endowment for the Arts, a federal agency.

The following stories were published in earlier versions: "Learn! Learn!" in *Revista Chicano-Riqueña,* VIII, 1, 1980; "Jitomates" in *Nuestro,* April, 1980; "Distillation" in *Chicago,* October, 1980; and "Ricardo's War" and "The Birthday Present" in *Revista Chicano-Riqueña,* XIII, 2, 1985.

Arte Publico Press
University of Houston
Houston, Texas 77004

Martínez-Serros, Hugo, 1930-
    The last laugh and other stories.

    Contents: The last laugh -- Her -- The birthday present -- [etc.]
    1. Mexican Americans--Illinois--Chicago--Fiction.
2. Chicago (Ill.)--fiction. I. Title.
PS3563.A73347L3   1988   813'.54   88-6359
ISBN 0-934770-89-1

Contents

The Last Laugh

Toward the end of April they moved a half block down the street to the big flat above Burley Liquors, one of several taverns in the neighborhood. They transformed the appearance of the building, dark and void upstairs for many years, by scrubbing the bluish grime from the second-floor windows and filling them with white curtains.

A warm spring made it unnecessary to heat the flat, and in the summer they thought only of keeping it cool. But in the fall, before the weather turned, José María Rivera spoke to Morris, the tavern keeper, about heating the building. "*Ya está*, it's settled," José María informed his wife, "we reached an agreement. We'll stoke the furnace and he'll buy the coal."

The Depression had made things difficult for José María. For years now he had been trying to pay off his debts, struggling to support a large family, and work was slow in the steel mills. With this move he had incurred another debt—the expense of repairing a flat that had been abandoned and run-down for years, a gathering place for bums and drunks who did not always relieve themselves in the toilet.

The owner of the building, the Riveras' doctor, had refused to rent it out. It was a rattrap and he could not afford the extensive repairs it would take to make it habitable. But José María had pressed him so often—they were cramped for space in the flat they occupied—that Dr. Stern finally gave in to his proposition. He did it conditionally: the finished flat would have to pass the doctor's inspection. The whole family labored for weeks to repair the place, as if their very lives had depended on it. Soap, brushes, paint, varnish, wallpaper, windowpanes and so much more had forced José María to buy on credit. It was worth it. They made the spacious flat attractive and in the end José María was ahead since Dr. Stern had felt confused and guilty about how much the rent would be, and he wound up setting it at a pittance. Both men had profited from the arrangement. And this agreement with Morris was another victory for José María—it would save him a great deal of money.

Lázaro and Jaime learned of the agreement from their mother, looked at each other and smiled. They knew there would be more to it than just stoking the furnace. And they knew the furnace would be their responsibility once their father taught them how to take care of it. Jorge and Gabriel, their older brothers, had other responsibilities.

The first load of coal, six tons, came in mid-September. It was dumped in the alley—the cheapest delivery—and José María, Lázaro and Jaime got it into the coal bin in the basement. Jaime loaded up the wheelbarrow as high as he could and José María eased it through the gate in the backyard fence, along the narrow walk that led to the sunken staircase fitted with the chute José María had made for this very task, and dumped it. The coal plunged into the basement, landing in a pile outside the basement door. From there Lázaro shoveled it into a bin just inside the door.

Without surprise Lázaro and Jaime learned that laying in wood was part of the agreement. They needed solid pieces that would burn with sufficient intensity to ignite chunks of coal, enough to cover a great bed of interlocking cast-iron grates. They needed a winter's supply—enough to start a new fire every Saturday and to allow for mistakes. They did not have to hunt it down. José María's watchfulness spared them that. Old railroad ties were perfect and he had a knack for finding them, as if they were great magnets that pulled at him, steelworker that he was. The boys hauled them in their father's big iron-wheeled wagon, carried them into the basement, where one by one they went onto sawhorses to be reduced to blocks with a crosscut saw. The blocks were chopped with an axe. They kept a pile of wood against the wall and the axe rested in a block, its blade embedded in the dense grain.

Big as their furnace was, Lázaro and Jaime knew it was a toy to their father, a blast furnace keeper in the steel mill. He taught them the right way to start a fire, when and how to put the coal on, the importance of air. He taught them everything they needed to know about the furnace, stressing the importance of keeping it clean—free of clinkers, ashes and soot. And he taught them how to use the ashes to hold the heat at a certain level, to lower it, or to keep the fire burning long. Each night they banked the fire in the furnace, covered it with a blanket of ashes, to keep it going for eight or more hours until the following morning. Even in the coldest weather they could give Morris all the heat he wanted.

To reach the furnace Lázaro and Jaime had to enter the tavern. Morris kept the back door to the basement bolted from the inside. José María had not wanted his sons to go into the tavern, especially when it was crowded. He knew the neighborhood and its saloons and was wary of them. But Morris refused to leave the basement door open. Instead he promised that he would not let his customers bother the boys in any way. A man of his word, he rarely had to warn them about the boys, and seldom with more than a few words.

The first time Lázaro and Jaime entered the tavern, a customer turned to look at them and said, "Hey, Panchos, wha'cha doin' here?" The boys said nothing.

"Leave the kids alone," Morris told him, "they fire the furnace." It was late October and the boys entered the tavern self-consciously, heads lowered and eyes on the floor.

"Hey, Panchos," he said again, "wanna come home wit me an' fire my furnace? Yooze can sleep wit my dog."

"I said leave the kids alone, goddamnit!" Morris barked. "I'll Pancho your ass right outta here if you bother 'em again!"

7

"Awright, awright, don't get so hot," the man protested, "I was only kiddin'."

"You wanna kid someone, you kid me," Morris scolded.

It didn't take long for the customers to learn that Morris was committed to protecting the boys. And the boys gradually gained a degree of confidence when they entered the tavern, managing to hold their head up and look straight forward. Sometimes Morris asked them to raise or lower the heat and they obeyed him immediately. And when customers were friendly with the boys, Morris smiled.

"You kids gonna do good down there?" someone asked.

"Gonna try," one of the boys answered.

Once when Lázaro came in alone somebody asked him, "Hey kiddo, where'd you learn to fire like that?"

"My father showed me," Lázaro answered.

The man winked and told Morris, "Give the kid a beer or a pop, whatever he wants, on me. Go ahead kid, take it."

He asked for a pop and said, "Thank you, sir."

"Goddamn polite kid," another said. "Wish mine was like that. Way mos' kids avoid sayin' sir, you'd think it was poison or somethin'."

Even when the tavern was crowded and noisy, when people were dancing or moving from the bar to the tables and playing shuffleboard and pinball, Lázaro and Jaime could pass through the tavern with ease to get to the basement.

"Hey Harvey! I thought you said the furnace didn't work in cold weather. Nothin' wrong with it now!" a man at the bar said. It was the first cold day of winter and the temperature had fallen below freezing.

"Napier said it too!" another added. "I guess you guys forgot to tell them kids it was'n suppose' to work."

"Why'nt you bozos ask them kids how they do it?" a third kidded. "Jus' make sure you ask 'em real nice."

Neither rose to the taunts but sat quietly drinking beer. They worked in the tavern and lived in the flophouse across the street, ran errands for Morris, kept the tavern clean, did other chores. Morris fed them, gave them beer and a little pocket money, paid their rent. They were always around.

"Morris, hey Morris! Did'n I tell ya? It was'n the damn furnace!" someone at the bar yelled.

"Trouble with Napier's he was pokin' roun' innuh wrong furnace!" somebody explained.

Napier's nose twitched above his thin black moustache. He broke his silence and spoke up, "Chrissakes . . . can't a man . . . have a quiet drink aroun' here . . . widdout a buncha bastards ridin' him?" He had been drinking all afternoon, more than Harvey, and his speech and reflexes had slowed, but he kept his composure.

"Can't take the truth?" somebody asked.

"Can't take your shit," Harvey answered. "If the place was so goddamn cold, how come you guys were always here?"

"Listen to who's talkin'," somebody said, "the ole fireman hisself. Morris hadda help you bums out 'cause you let the furnace go out. You 'specially." Laughter exploded.

"Aw shut up! The whole buncha you," Harvey snapped. He was twice Napier's age, his face broad and purpled by years of drinking, his nose a large drying plum, his tired eyes buried in baggy folds.

"Hey Morris, tell these jokers! Did'n we freeze our ass off in here las' winter?" Morris smiled, said nothing.

Harvey finished his beer and stood up. "Buncha shitheads, alla you. Worse'n babies," he muttered as he shambled to the door. They jeered him, laughed and whistled. He turned up his coat collar and pulled down the bill of the greasy cap he never took off, strands of lank gray hair showing at his ears. He was Morris' favorite errand boy and all-around handyman, a better and more dependable worker than Napier. Wherever he went he infected the air with the faint, lingering, unmistakable smell of piss.

For Napier and Harvey the Riveras, Lázaro and Jaime in particular, were intruders in the basement, in the tavern, upstairs. Napier, of an age with José María, was everything he was not, and he and Harvey greeted him indifferently and stayed out of his way. Before the coming of the Riveras they would gather upstairs with their friends to drink pint and half-pint bottles of wine, whiskey, brandy, gin, whatever they could get. José María found empty bottles strewn everywhere in the flat. Napier and Harvey had controlled entry to the flat and had enjoyed a certain standing among the neighborhood drunks. And they had held a certain advantage over Morris in the winter, when firing the furnace became important. They lost all this with the coming of the Riveras.

Burley Liquors was open seven days a week, from early morning until after midnight. Lázaro and Jaime grew accustomed to entering it, yet they never forgot it was a man's world, a place for adults, for tough women. There, voices were loud, laughter raucous, the air thick with cigarette smoke and the reek of alcohol and the foulest language they had ever heard. It was a place that made them feel like intruders, that admitted them grudgingly. They were quick to spot a hostile eye, to see bodies stiffen at their entry, to detect disapproving silences. But Morris was there—short, thickset, massive, like a bulldog, the bulldog on the nose of a Mack truck or the truck itself—and they knew they were safe. Joyless and scowling, he opened the tavern every morning and worked until he closed it at night and padlocked the iron curtain across the front of the building. He controlled everything in the tavern, kept it clean, and barked orders at Harvey and Napier. Once, Lázaro and Jaime saw him pull out his gun and lay it on the bar in front of him when a customer started arguing with him.

10

It took the Riveras a while to get used to their new surroundings. At night the sound of voices and the jukebox kept them awake. Sometimes dancing would start up suddenly and the stamping of feet would awaken them. In time all this became familiar to them, assumed a rhythm that lulled them to sleep at night. At times they hummed or whistled in harmony with the jukebox; sometimes they danced to its music. There came a day, finally, when only a break in the usual nightly rhythm—shouting or fighting—awakened them.

On Saturdays Morris got to the tavern at six in the morning. It was his longest, busiest day. Harvey and Napier got there at seven and worked to Morris' commands—sweeping, mopping, dusting, washing, straightening, filling, stacking, emptying, back and forth they went at a slow pace that the tavern keeper's unrelenting snapping could not quicken.

At eight o'clock when the tavern opened, earlier if it was very cold, Lázaro and Jaime made their entry. Saturday was their big day too. From the moment the boys appeared, Harvey and Napier grumbled from behind mop and broom, and if there was no one in the tavern, they could be worse than any customer. Morris' presence did not intimidate the two men.

"Fuckin' Mexicans trackin' up the floor!" the old man howled without looking at them when they boys got close.

"Shut up, damn you!" Morris ordered. "Their father ever hears you he'll break your neck!" Then he turned on the boys, "What are you waiting for? Tell him off! Don't jus' stand there'n let him get away with it!" The boys remained silent; his presence restrained them. It annoyed him.

"Lousy spics dirtyin' the floor!" the old man went on. "I jus' finished moppin' it, you little bastards!"

"Mop it again, you skunk! Stinky ole skunk!" Jaime

exploded. "You need a bath! Try usin' that mop on yourself!"

"Piss pot!" Lázaro hissed. "Dirty ole piss pot!"

Morris laughed. He was a practical joker who hated hostility and threw out anyone who fought or threatened to fight in the tavern.

"Smart aleck pun . . . punks!" Napier suddenly said, coming to Harvey's aid. When he got angry or excited he stuttered. "I'll be . . . beat yer . . . yer ass yer ole . . . ole lady won't know you!" He moved toward them and the boys stopped and turned to face him. He stopped too. They had talked about Napier many times. Together they were not afraid of him. They were sure that, together, they could handle him.

"Boozer, dumb boozer!" Jaime spat at him.

"Can't even talk straight, you booze hound!" Lázaro jeered.

Napier raised his broom and Morris growled, "Enough, goddamn-it, enough!" stepping between them.

The boys moved on but saw Morris smile. They heard him laugh as they turned left at the jukebox, opened the door and made their way down the stairs. Behind his laughter they heard the angry complaints of the two men. They had to pass through Harvey's and Napier's part of the basement to get to the other end, their end.

In pails, boxes and heaps to one side of the furnace were the ashes and clinkers the furnace had given up during the week. Boxes and pails of clinkers and ashes were carried to the alley and dumped there in neat piles the garbage men would shovel onto their truck. Back and forth the two went until the floor was cleared.

When they finished their chores upstairs, Harvey and Napier went down to the basement to clean up the mess they had made in the course of the week. "I don't want any fightin' down there, unnerstand? No arguin' with them kids for nothin'. Jus' stay on your side," Morris warned them. He waited at the top of the stairs until he heard them start to work and then returned to the bar. Down there they were their own boss. They tied cardboard into bundles, matched empty bottles with empty cases, stacked a week's supply of beer, seltzer and pop within easy reach, swept up broken glass and other debris, ending their labors by hosing down the concrete floor. Morris descended briefly to inspect what they had done.

At the other extremity the boys continued to work. They were ten and eleven and a half years old and could do some things as well as grown men. Lázaro, who was older, chopped wood off to one side, away from Jaime. When he finished he began to shovel coal into place for the coming week. Jaime cleaned the furnace, the most important job. He started with the clinkers, extracting them from the furnace carefully, long poker and tongs alternating, digging deep to dislodge thick, heavy, red-hot deposits encrusted like plaque on the massive toothy grates. If it was very cold the trick was to make the extractions little by little and with minimal loss of the heat's intensity; otherwise it was faster and easier to start a new fire. With a long metal rake Jaime removed the ashes from the big bed under the grates, the flat rectangular head moving across the base of the furnace until only the clean sound of metal scraping metal could be heard. With a smaller rake he cleaned the soot from the upper part of the furnace, the dark flue that blued with flickering, elongated flames. Like Napier and Harvey, the boys hosed down their end of the basement when they finally finished.

Before noon, Jaime and Lázaro emerged from the basement, their faces flushed, their eyes shining. "All through down there?" Morris asked. "Yes sir," they would answer.

Eating a sandwich and drinking beer, Harvey and Napier sat at the bar. They did not turn to look at the boys, said nothing. Morris was there. To himself Napier cursed the Riveras. Their invasion of the upstairs flat had put an end to his opportunities to drink hard liquor. Neighborhood drunks no longer shared their bottles with him and Harvey as they had when the flat was empty. Now he had to settle for the glasses of beer Morris served him as part of his pay; he never served him anything stronger. And those punks had taken over his basement too. He and Harvey had talked about it; Harvey saw it the same way. He turned to the old man, who looked at him and shook his head. Harvey hated the little bastards for not respecting his age. No good spics. And to think they were important just because they stoked the furnace. Damn him, it was Morris' fault. Defended them and ordered him and Napier around like children, made them work more now. The door closed behind them and Harvey muttered, "Git the hell outta here an' don't come back."

Lázaro and Jaime called him Napier the Raper. In the basement under the stairs there was a bed built on sawhorses—a door layered with cardboard and old blankets. It could not be seen from the top of the stairway even when the light was on. Napier and Harvey took turns napping there—Napier on his back, nose pointed straight up, his trousers neatly hung on a nail overhead; Harvey snoring noisily, cap on his head, his dirty bunioned feet freed of shoes and socks. But on weekends when the tavern was crowded, Napier the Raper and certain customers sometimes did other things there. The boys, entering the basement unexpectedly, had caught them at it more than once. They would laugh, whisper and look toward the bed without letting up until the pair finally left. Morris never held the boys back, never said anything to them, but only flashed a lewd smile, rolled his eyes, made clicking sounds with his tongue, knowing what they would find down there. They learned to read his face.

Napier had tried to run them out of the basement on

those occasions by threatening them, cursing them; they had responded by laughing and returning his threats. In spite of all his companion's urging, Napier had not dared to approach them when they armed themselves with axe and poker and beckoned him with a motion of their arm. But if he was down there, Lázaro and Jaime never took their eyes from him. Harvey was another matter; down there he ignored them completely and they didn't even bother to look at him.

Sometimes Napier and Harvey quarreled and Lázaro and Jaime found out about it because Harvey would not leave the tavern until it closed, and he would return in the morning before Morris arrived and wait on the Rivera's doorstep. When it happened, Harvey did not speak to Napier, and if the opportunity arose he would side with the boys against him: "Tell the son-of-a-bitch to kiss yer ass! Don't be afraid of him!" But their quarrel never lasted more than a couple of days and then the old man became their enemy again.

Time passed and Lázaro and Jaime lost their self-consciousness about entering the tavern. They would make their way through it slowly now. One of them might drop something deliberately and pause to retrieve it, or he might pause to show the other something. And they tarried at the occurrence of something interesting. Now they would often take turns firing the furnace.

The basement became their favorite retreat when it was too cold to play outside. It was far better than staying at home. Down there they had discovered a private world, one whose darkness engulfed everything except the bright shafts that escaped from the furnace, a darkness that lost its density at the flick of a switch and receded to places where it could hide. It was a world where nobody could take them by surprise. With the slightest pressure the stairs creaked and the back door was held fast with a crossbar. Supported by raw beams that heat and time had made porous, the low ceiling, underside of the floor upstairs, was a tangle of exposed planks and braces bristling with nails, strung with the branching nerves of electrical wires, lanced and clamped to hold rusting pipes like flaking bones. Tattered nets of dusty cobwebs were everywhere. Water oozed from leprous pipes and made dark stains on the cracked, peeling walls that were sunken here, swollen there. And everywhere there were cases of pop, seltzer and beer, and empty bottles. All this was familiar and reassuring to the two boys. They did not know it, but the tavern and everything about it had drawn them into a deep alliance.

"Come on, don't be a baby! There's no one aroun', they're all busy upstairs," Lázaro urged.

"You go first if you're so brave!" Jaime responded.

After daring one another several times, one of the boys would pry off the cap of a small bottle of beer—one overlooked in an empty case—and together they would drink it in the darkened basement. Both hated the bitter liquid, yet each thought the other liked it, and both drank quickly, each eager to pass the bottle to the other. While the beer lasted, their apprehension amplified the footsteps on the floor right above and directed them to the door that led to the basement.

Sometimes they turned seltzer bottles into guns, firing squirts of charged water that rose from the dregs. And they became targets for one another. But their favorite target was the furnace. Squeezing the release, they made the metal nozzles attached to the heavy bottles spurt seltzer at the furnace, the liquid exploding on contact and disappearing. Sometimes they took turns on the basement bed, moving in exaggerated imitation of Napier the Raper struggling over some victim. And there were times when they labored with great care to remove an enormous red-hot clinker from the furnace, strained to set it on the floor without breaking it, and then gleefully aimed cautious jets of urine at it from a safe distance, jumping back as the deep sizzle filled the basement with great clouds of acrid steam that made them cough and shed tears. Morris' barking always brought them back to reality, "Hey! What's goin' on down there? What's that goddamn stink? Cut it out or I'll tell your ole man when I see him!" They stood silently beside the clinker that had turned deep shades of gray, blue, purple, its appearance strikingly metallic, almost lustrous, like a strange piece of coral from outer space.

On a morning in late January, before going to school, Lázaro and Jaime fired the furnace as they did every morning. To his surprise Jaime found a case of beer just outside the back door to the basement—he had opened it to retrieve a shovel left there the day before. On their way out they told Morris about the beer.

They did not hear Morris rage, accuse Napier and Harvey of stealing from him, threaten to turn them in to the police. He drove them from the tavern and barred them for a week, took them back only when they paid for the beer as punishment for their dishonesty and assured him repeatedly that it was their only disloyalty to him ever. They had run out of money and were going to celebrate Napier's birthday with two girlfriends. But everything had gone wrong and they were unable to return for the beer.

For weeks Napier and Harvey rankled, looking for a way to get even with the boys—weeks of outrageous obscenities exchanged by the four. Morris laughed through it all; he had taught the two men a lesson. And then came the chance to retaliate that Napier and Harvey longed for. In a moment of madness inspired by a movie they had seen, Lázaro and Jaime took full bottles of seltzer to enact a shoot-out. They doused one another, hit everything in sight, hissed furious jets into the farthest corners. Napier, intrigued by the noises coming from the basement, sneaked up on Lázaro and Jaime and caught them in the heat of battle. He denounced them to Morris. Morris reviled them and reported them to José María. José María paid for the seltzer. In the basement, in the presence of Morris and Napier, he made Lázaro and Jaime apologize. Then he whipped them without mercy and had them mop up the floor.

For weeks Napier and Harvey gloated, laughed, rubbed the boys' noses into their humiliation: "Pricks! Sassy little bastards! Thought you was so fuckin' smart! Tole you we'd get even with yer spic asses!" The boys kept a dense silence and entered the basement only to fire the furnace and to clean up on Saturdays.

One day the weather dropped below zero and Lázaro and Jaime had to stoke the furnace frequently to keep an intense fire burning. When they opened the furnace door an infernal blast would drive them back and they could feel the heat sear their faces, seeming to singe eyebrows and lashes. They wore leather gloves to work with the long poker, the tongs, the big coal shovel. Clinkers formed with irksome speed and had to be removed. They worked in spurts, backing off because hands, face and thighs could not stand the heat. At night Lázaro banked; in the morning Jaime awaited Morris' arrival. And when they were in school José María fired. For the boys the days were a single day that kept repeating itself.

It was still very cold early Saturday morning when the boys went downstairs. Harvey and Napier mocked them, but they did not answer. They entered the basement, stoked the furnace and left. Upstairs they were helping their father repair a linen closet. At nine Lázaro returned to the basement to fire the furnace again and at ten-thirty Jaime took his turn. Just before noon the two were back in the basement doing their chores. Working together or taking turns, they removed clinkers little by little, extracting as many as the scorching heat would allow, trying to maintain the fire's intensity. They worked at a steady pace, avoiding unnecessary trips to the alley, opening the back door only when they had to. Like Napier and Harvey, they shunned the cold.

It was Jaime who noticed them, their shape just visible in the shadows under the stairs. They were lying on the bed, waiting for him, beckoning to him—two winter coats, Harvey's and Napier's. They never left them there, had them on that morning when he and Lázaro entered the tavern, which was always a bit cool before the furnace was stoked. The two men had gone to the basement—the warmest place in the building—wearing them, worked for a time, shed them when they felt hot, and left them there when they finished their chores. What else could explain their being there? Jaime knew that for the rest of the day the weather would keep Harvey and Napier seated at the bar, where they were drinking beer at that very moment.

Jaime went to them, picked them up with his fingertips as if he feared contagion, and brought them into the light. "Look," he said handing one to Lázaro. They held them up for inspection. By degrees, turning them, searching them, poking them, they became more familiar with them. Then Jaime smiled, slipped the coat on and began to mimic Napier. At once Lázaro joined him. They shuffled, muttered incoherently, did bumps and grinds, stumbled and staggered and mumbled, all the while stifling and muffling their laughter.

What followed happened suddenly. Lázaro has always insisted that it was Jaime's idea to do what they did. Jaime took off the coat and threw it on the chopping block. Then he took up the axe, raised it high and brought it down on the garment, cutting through it. His eyes hard and shining, he looked at Lázaro, smiled and began swinging the axe viciously, stopping only to stifle his laughter. And then Lázaro pulled off his coat and flung it on top of the other. He took the axe from Jaime and began to chop with short, well-aimed blows and then gradually lengthened the radius of his swing and the blade sliced the air savagely, cutting it into great arcs before falling on the coats without mercy, slashing through them to the block whose dense grain caught and held it after every blow. Lost in their frenzied ritual—their memory would keep it forever vivid—they took turns swinging the axe with undiminished vigor, repeatedly, hacking away at the garments again and again and stifling their laughter over and over, not letting up until they had shredded the coats. Spent, Lázaro sat down on a wooden box. Jaime reached for a broom and swept up the remains. Lázaro watched him, then he got up quickly, opened the furnace door, grabbed a shovel and pitched in all traces of their deed. They hurried to finish their chores, abandoned the basement and passed quietly through the tavern.

They did not go upstairs, but fled instead to the corner and turned it. Vapor clung to their faces when they exhaled, but they did not feel the cold. There was no one in sight; they could express themselves freely. They reached the big oak tree. Naked of its summer leaves, it was no longer imposing. There they burst into uproarious laughter, slapping and kicking the tree without restraint, laughed and laughed, tears running down their faces, until they could laugh no more.

Distillation

He went on Saturdays because it was the best day. He did it for years and we, his sons, were his helpers. And yet one day alone remains, that single distant Saturday—a day so different from the rest that I cannot forget it.

Friday night I was in bed by nine. It would take us about an hour to get there and we had to leave by eight the following morning to arrive just before the first tall trucks. All day the trucks would come and go, all day until five in the afternoon. My father wanted to get there before anyone else. He wanted to look it all over and then swoop down on the best places. There the spoils would go to the quickest hands and we would work in swift thrusts, following his example, obeying the gestures and words he used to direct us.

That Saturday morning my father waited impatiently for us, his piercing whistles shrilling his annoyance at our delay. Anxious for us, my mother pushed us through the door as she grazed us with her lips. My father was flicking at his fingers with a rag and turned sharply to glower at us. I saw fresh grease on the hubs of the big iron wheels that supported the weight of his massive wagon, its great wooden bed and sides fixed on heavy steel axletrees. He spoke harshly to us, for we had kept him waiting and he was angry: "¡*Con un mierda!* Goddammit! What the hell took you so long? ¡*Vámonos!*"

He had already lowered the wagon's sides. Now, grasping us at the armpits, he picked us up and set us in beside the burlap sacks and a bag of food, starting with me, the youngest, and following the order of our ages—five, six and a half, eight and eleven. He handed us a gallon jug of water and then pulled the *guayín* through the door in the backyard fence, easing it out into the alley by the very long shaft that was its handle, like some vaguely familiar giant gently drawing a ship by its prow.

Yawning in the warmth of May, I leaned back, like my brothers, in anticipation of the joys of a crossing that would reach almost a full length of the longest line that could be drawn in the world as I knew it. That world, dense and more durable than a name, extended just beyond South Chicago. The day, a vast blue balloon stretched to its limits by a great flood of light, contained us and invited our blinking eyes to examine all that it enveloped.

The fastest route led us down alleys, away from pedestrians, cars, trucks and wide horse-drawn wagons that plied the streets. The alleys, always familiar, seemed somehow new in the morning light that gleamed on piles of garbage and everywhere flashed slivers of rainbows in beads of moisture. Garbage men used shovels to clear away these piles. What garbage cans there were stood sheltered against walls and fences or lay fallen in heaps of refuse. Through the unpaved alleys we went, over black earth hard-packed and inlaid with myriad fragments of glass that sparkled in the morning radiance. Ahead of us rats scattered, fleeing the noise and bulk that moved toward them. Stray dogs, poking their noses into piles, did not retreat at our approach. Sunlight and shadows mottled my vision as the wagon rolled past trees, poles, fences, garages, sheds. My father moved in and out of the light, in and out of the shadows. On clotheslines threadbare garments waved and swelled. Without slowing down, my father navigated around potholes and these sudden maneuvers shook loose squeals and laughter as our bodies swayed.

At 86th Street he had to leave the alleys to continue south. There the steel mills and train yards suddenly closed in on us. We rattled over the railroad crossing at Burley Avenue, a busy, noisy pass, and this made me stiffen and press my palms against my ears. For one block Burley Avenue was a corridor—the only one for some distance around—that allowed movement north and south. At 89th Street my father followed a southwestern course, going faster and faster, farther and farther from the steel mills, moving beyond the commercial area into a zone where the houses looked more and more expensive and the lawns grew thicker and greener. Already there were many flowers here, but no noise and few children, and there were no alleys. As my father rushed through these neighborhoods we fell silent. I was baffled by the absence of garbage and my eyes searched for an explanation that was to remain hidden from me for years.

At the end of a street that advanced between rows of brick bungalows stood the tunnel. We entered it and I tensed, at once exhilarated and alarmed by the wagon's din, frightened by the sudden darkness yet braving it because my father was there. A long time passed before we reached midpoint, where I feared everything would cave in on us. Then slowly my father's silhouette, pillar like, filled the space ahead of me, growing larger and larger as we approached the light. Beyond the tunnel there were no houses and we emerged into the radiance of 95th Street and Torrence Avenue.

There, stopping for the traffic that raced along 95th Street, my father quickly harnessed himself to the wagon with the double rope that was coiled around its prowlike handle. He was safe in this rude harness, for he could loosen it instantly and drop back alongside the great vehicle to brake it if the need arose. Now he pulled his wagon into Torrence Avenue and his legs pumped, hard at first and then they let up and soon he was running. Torrence Avenue, broad and well paved, shone like still water and he ran smoothly, with long strides, at about three-quarters of his top speed. We were smiling now and we saw the smile on his face when he looked back over his shoulder. Breathing easily he ran before us and I watched his effortless movement forward. I felt a sudden keen desire to be just like him and for an instant found it difficult to breathe. To our right was a green expanse—trees, wild flowers, grasses and a bountiful variety of weeds—like a green sea extending to the horizon. Torrence Avenue now curved gently to the left for half a block and farther ahead gradually straightened along a stretch of several blocks, flanked on the left by a high fence and a long dense row of poplars. As my father navigated out of the curve we urged him on.

"Faster, Pa, faster! ¡*Más rápido*!"

"Come on, Pa, you c'n go faster'n that!"

"Pa, as fast as you c'n go, Pa, as fast as you c'n go!"

"Like a car, Pa, like a car!"

The prow shot forward, chasing my father as he reached top speed and the craft darted into the straight lane that would take us to 103rd Street. My heart unleashed and racing, I looked up into the row of trees at the shoreline, saw swift islets of blue sky coursing brightly through the green current of foliage. Along the shoreline my father's pace gradually slowed until he seemed to be moving at half speed. Whenever he glanced backward we saw sweat trickling down his forehead and following the line of his eyebrows to join the streamlets running from his temples. Beads of perspiration swelled at his hairline and slid down his neck into the blue-denim shirt, which deepened to a dolphin color. Far beyond the fence, their smoking stacks thrust into the sky, the steel mills took on the appearance of enormous, dark, steam-driven vessels.

At 103rd Street my father veered due west. Ahead of us, at a distance of several blocks, loomed the 103rd Street Bridge. All his pacing had led to this, was a limbering up for this ascent. Many yards before the street rose, my father began to increase his speed with every stride. He did it gradually, never slackening, for the wagon was heavy and accelerated slowly. I placed the gallon jug of water between my legs and tightened them around it as he reached full speed just before storming the incline. He started up unfalteringly, tenaciously, with short rapid steps and his body bent forward, his natural reaction to the exaggerated resistance suddenly offered by the wagon. From a point high in the sky the pavement poured down on us. Immediately my father was drenched in sweat. His face, in profile now on the left, now on the right, became twisted with exertion while his broad back grew to twice its size under the strain. We held our breath, maintained a fragile silence and did not move, our bodies taut from participation in his struggle. All the way up we lost speed by degrees. His breathing grew heavy, labored. His legs slowed, seeking now to recover with more powerful thrusts what they had lost with a diminished number of strokes. His jaw tightened, his head fell, sometimes he closed his eyes and could see his tortured face as his arms swung desperately at some invisible opponent and still he went up, up, up.

When the pavement leveled off he yielded for a moment, broke into a smile and then, summoning reserves from the labyrinth of his will, lunged forward furiously, as if galvanized by his victory, and reached full speed at the moment the wagon began to descend. Miraculously, he freed himself from the harness, turned the shaft back into the wagon and jumped on. Winking at us he fell to his knees and leaned hard on the shaft. He was happy, wildly happy, and saw that we were too and he laughed without restraint. "*Miren, vean*, look around you!" he shouted to us.

We were at the summit and the world fell away from us far into the horizon. To the east, steel mills, granaries, railroad yards, a profusion of industrial plants; to the north and south, prairies, trees, some houses; to the west, main arteries, more plants, the great smoking heaps of the city dump, and, farther still, houses and a green sweep of trees that extended as far as the eye saw. Years have changed this area in many ways, but that landscape, like a photo negative, glows in memory's light.

We had churned up the mountainous wave of the bridge, and now, as we coasted down ever faster, we screeched and I could feel my body pucker. Our excitement was different now. It came of expectancy, of the certain knowledge that we would soon be sailing. We were safe with our incomparable pilot, but we howled with nervous delight as we picked up speed. Down, down, straight down we fell, and then the *guayín* righted itself and my stomach shot forward, threatening for a fraction of a second to move beyond its body.

When the wagon finally came to a stop my father got down. Again he harnessed himself to it and pulled us onward. He moved with haste but did not run. Looking into the immense blue dome above us we knew our journey would soon end and we began to shift uneasily, anticipating our arrival. With cupped hands we covered our faces and grew silent while the wheels beneath us seemed to clack-clack louder and louder each time they passed over the pavement lines. At the divided highway my father turned south. We would be there in minutes.

The wagon stopped. We dropped our hands, exposing our faces, and climbed down. The full stink of decomposing garbage, fused to that of slow-burning trash, struck us. Before us was the city dump—a great raw sore on the landscape, a leprous tract oozing flames and smoldering, hellish grounds columned in smoke and grown tumid across years. Fragments of glass, metal, wood lay everywhere, some of them menacingly jagged where they had not been driven into the earth by the wheels of the ponderous trucks.

My father had learned that the dump yielded more and better on Saturdays. Truckloads of spoiled produce were dumped that day, truckloads from warehouses, markets, stores, truckloads of stale or damaged food. We would spend the entire day here, gathering, searching, sifting, digging, following the trucks' shifting centers of activity.

Along a network of roads that crisscrossed the dumping grounds, trucks lumbered to and fro, grinding forward over ruts, jerking backward, all of them rocking from side to side. My father took some burlap sacks, scanned the area and pointed to the site where we would work. He went toward it quickly, followed by my oldest brothers. Lázaro and I stationed the wagon beyond reach of the clumsy vehicles that were already dumping and then made our way to the site. We started to work on a huge pile of deteriorating fruit, picking only what a paring knife would later make edible.

After several trips to the wagon my father and brothers moved on to other piles. My job was to stay and guard the wagon, neatly arranging all that went into it. When I remembered, I took the jug of water and buried it in the earth to keep it cool. Eager for their company, I waited for my brothers to return with their newest finds.

From where I stood guard I could see my father and brothers hurrying toward a truck that had just arrived. It was rumbling toward a dump area just beyond me. The men on that high, wobbly truck were pointing, nodding, waving—gestures signaling my father and brothers to follow because they carried a rich load. Directed by a man who advanced slowly and seemed to walk on his knees, the truck waded into a heap of garbage, dumped its cargo to the whir of a hydraulic mechanism and was pulling out as my father and brothers drew close enough to express their gratitude with a slight movement of their heads.

Now my father waved to me. It was a call to join them before others arrived. As I started toward them my brother Lázaro foundered on a spongy mass, fell through it and disappeared. I stopped in my tracks, stunned. "Buried," I whispered, "he's buried!" My father saw him fall, bolted to his side and thundered a command, "*Alzate*, Lázaro, get up, get up!" and in seconds he had raised him. Unsteady on his feet, Lázaro shook himself off like a wet dog and then brushed away scabs of rotting stuff that clung to him. Suddenly the stench of decay, the idea of grabbing something that might crumble into muck, the thought of losing my footing in all that garbage, filled me with terror. On tentative feet I went forward cautiously, expecting the ground to give way beneath me. My steps were becoming steady when one of them set off a long, frenzied squeak. A rat sprang from under my foot and retreated grudgingly, black eyes unblinking, sharp teeth flashing beneath bristly whiskers, long tail stiffly trailing its fat body. I did not move until my father's shrill whistle roused me; then he called me in an angry voice and I moved on.

Working in silence we gathered what we wanted from that mound. Now and again the sun's oppressive heat was dimmed by clouds that seemed to come from nowhere, bringing us relief.

By noon the sky was overcast. We pulled the wagon away from the dumping area and sat on the ground to eat what we had brought from home. By then the stench no longer bothered us. My father handed us bean and potato tacos that were still warm. Hunger made them exquisite and I sat there chewing slowly, deliberately, making them last, too happy to say anything. We shared the jug of water, bits of damp earth clinging to our hands after we set it down.

Before us was the coming and going of trucks, the movement of men, rats scurrying everywhere, some dogs and just beyond us, under a tent-like tarp, a big gas-powered pump that was used to drain water from that whole area, which flooded easily in a heavy rain. Behind us was a tiny shack, crudely assembled with cardboard, wood and sheet metal, home of the dump's only dweller, Uñas. He was nowhere in sight, but my mind saw him—a monstrous dung beetle rolling balls endlessly, determination on his pockmarked face, jaws in constant motion and his hands thrashing nervously, searching the grounds with a frenzy unleashed by the appearance of intruders.

By 12:30 the sky's blue was completely eclipsed. Above us an ugly gray was pressing down the sky, flattening it by degrees. My father stood up and looked hard at the sky as he spun on his heel. The temperature dropped abruptly and a strong wind rose, blowing paper, cans, boxes and other objects across the grounds in all directions. He issued orders rapidly: "¡*Pronto!* Block the wheels and cover the wagon with the *lona*! Tie it down!" Then he took a sack and hurried off to a heap he had been eyeing while we ate.

He leaped forward, the two youngest scurrying in search of something to anchor the wheels with while the two eldest raised the wagon's sides and unfolded the tarp my father had designed for such an emergency. The wheels blocked, we turned to help our brothers. We had seen our father tie down the tarp many times. We pulled it taut over the wagon and carefully drew the ends down and under, tying securely the lengths of rope that hung from its edges.

Huddled around the wagon, we watched the day grow darker. Big black clouds, their outlines clearly visible, scudded across the sky. It was cold and we shivered in our shirt sleeves. Now the wind blew with such force that it lifted things and flung them into spasmodic flight. We moved in together and bent down to shield and anchor ourselves. Frightened, we held our silence and pressed in closer until one of us, pointing, gasped, "Look! No one's out there! No one! Jus' look! We're all alone!"

A bolt of lightening ripped the sky and a horrendous explosion followed. Terror gripped us and we began to wail.

The clouds dumped their load of huge, cold drops. And suddenly my father appeared in the distance. He looked tiny as he ran flailing his arms, unable to shout over the sound of wind and water. He was waving us into the shack and we obeyed at once. Inside, cowed by the roar outside and pressing together, we trembled as we waited for him. He had almost reached us when the wind sheared off the roof. Part of one side was blown away as the first small pebbles of ice began to fall. He was shouting as he ran, "*Salgan*, come out, come out!"

We tumbled out, arms extended as we groped toward him, clutched his legs when he reached us and pulled us away seconds before the wind leveled what remained of the shack. A knot of arms and legs, we stumbled to the wagon. There was no shelter for hundreds of yards around and we could not see more than several yards in front of us. The rain slashed down, diminished, and hail fell with increasing density as the size of the spheres grew. Now we cried out with pain as white marbles struck us. My father's head pitched furiously and he bellowed with authority, "¡*Cállense*!" Be still! Don't move from here! I'll be right back, *ahorita vuelvo*!"

In seconds he was back, dragging behind him the huge tarp he had torn from the pump, moving unflinchingly under the cold jawbreakers that were pummeling us. With a powerful jerk he pulled it up his back and over his head, held out his arms like wings and we instinctively darted under. The growing force of the hailstorm crashed down on him. Thrashing desperately under the tarp we found his legs and clung to them. I crawled between them. We could not stop bawling.

Once more he roared over the din, "¡*Con una chingada, cállense*! There's nothing to fear! ¡*Nada*! You're safe with me, you know that, *ya lo saben*!" And then little by little he lowered his voice until he seemed to be whispering, "I would never let anything harm you, *nunca, nunca. Ya, cállense, cállense ya. Cálmense*, be still, you're safe, *seguros*, you're with me, with *Papá*. It's going to end now, very soon, very soon, it'll end, you'll see, *ya verán, ya verán*. Be still, be still, you're with me, with me. *Ya, ya, cállense . . .* "

Bent forward he held fast, undaunted, fixed to the ground, and we tried to cast off our terror. Huddled under the wings of that spreading giant we saw the storm release its savagery, hurl spheres of ice like missiles shot from slings. They came straight down, so dense that we could see only a few feet beyond us. Gradually the storm abated and we watched the spheres bounce with great elasticity from hard surfaces, carom when they collided, spring from the wagon's tarp like golf balls dropped on blacktopped streets. When it stopped hailing, the ground lay hidden under a vast white beaded quilt. At a distance from us and down, the highway was a string of stationary vehicles with their lights on. Repeatedly, bright bolts of lightning tore the sky from zenith to horizon and set off detonations that seemed to come from deep in the earth. At last the rain let up. My father straightened himself, rose to his full height and we emerged from the tarp as it slid from his shoulders. He ordered us with a movement of his head and eyes and as he calmly flexed his arms the four of us struggled to cover the damaged pump with his great canvas mantle.

His unexpected "¡*Vámonos!*" filled us with joy and we prepared to leave. Hail and water were cleared from the wagon's cover. My brothers and I dug through the ice to free the wheels, and when my father took up the handle and pulled, we pushed from behind with all our might, slipping, falling, rising, moving the wagon forward by inches, slowly gaining a little speed and finally holding at a steady walk to keep from losing control. Where the road met the highway we waded through more than a foot of water and threw our shoulders into the wagon to shove it over the last bump. Long columns of stalled cars lined the highway as drivers examined dents and shattered or broken windows and windshields. We went home in a dense silence, my father steering and pulling in front, we propelling from behind.

Entering the yard from the alley, we unloaded the wagon without delay. While my father worked his wagon into the coal shed and locked the door, my brothers and I carried the sacks up to our second floor flat. It was almost four when we finished emptying the sacks on newspapers spread on the kitchen floor. There we began to pare while my mother, scrubbing carefully, washed in the sink. We chattered furiously, my brothers and I, safe now from the danger outside.

Lázaro brought the knife down on the orange, the orange slipped from his hand and the blade cut the tip of his thumb. He held his thumb in his fist and I got up to bring him gauze and tape from the bathroom. I knew my father would let me in even if he had already started to bathe.

Some object fallen between the bathroom door and its frame had kept it ajar, but he did not hear me approach. I froze. He was standing naked beside a heap of clothes, running his hands over his arms and shoulders, his fingertips pausing to examine more closely. His back and arms were a mass of ugly welts, livid flesh that had been flailed again and again until the veins beneath the skin had broken. His arms dropped to his sides and I thought I saw him shudder. Suddenly he seemed to grow, to swell, to fill the bathroom with his great mass. Then he threw his head back shaking his black mane, smiled, stepped into the bathtub and immersed himself in the water. Without knowing why, I waited a moment before timidly entering—even as I have paused all these years, and pause still, in full knowledge now, before entering that distant Saturday.

Her

You open your eyes before the alarm clock in the kitchen goes off. You roll onto your back and lie there, looking up at the ceiling and thinking about her, wondering again if all they say about her is really true, hoping they've made a lot of it up. All summer long you've thought about her and now the summer is over and you must face her, be with her.

Your day starts and you are nervous. You draw back the cotton spread, swing out your thin legs and sit on the edge of your cot. You pull on your socks, close your eyes momentarily, then stand up and step into your knickers. You sit down now, slip on your shoes and lace them.

There is no one in the bathroom; the others are still asleep. You plug the basin with a wash cloth, fill it with cold water from both faucets and submerge your hands. Slowly you soap your hands, then your face, rinse carefully and dry yourself. When you pull the wash cloth the drain swallows the water noisily, leaving a scummy film. You wash the basin and your hands, pour toothpowder into your cupped palm, stick your wet index finger into it and then rub your teeth vigorously. You dip your finger repeatedly, rubbing until you feel smoothness between finger and teeth, until the powder is gone. Now you fill your mouth with water, swelling your cheeks as you work the water round and round. Then you spit it out and smile, pleased with the sweet taste.

In the kitchen the alarm sounds. You reach it before your mother. When you finish dressing you will have more than enough time to eat and get your things ready. Summer's end doesn't sadden you—like school. But you feel uneasy about her. What will happen to you today? You wonder.

Outside the school you mill with the others, renew

friendships, exchange stories, anticipate the return to discipline and routine. The first bell rings. You enter the building and go directly to your classroom on the second floor. A girl posted just inside the room at the door to the cloakroom, which is closed, won't let you go in to hang up your sweater. "Get away," she says, "you can't go in there. She's changin' her clothes an' doesn't want no one peekin' at her." Her voice threatens, crackles with new power and authority. They are the same words she aims at those who come later. At the back of the class a second girl guards the other cloakroom door.

Buttoning the smock she wears over her skirt and blouse, she comes out before the last bell rings and stands in front of her desk. She is tall, strong-looking, has her hands on her hips and scowls at the boys who dare look at her. She jerks up her right hand and begins firing her index finger at every boy in the classroom, emphasizing the gesture with one word: "You! . . . You! . . . You! . . . " When she has singled all of you out she pauses, then she suddenly steps forward and shoots a warning, "Just let me catch one of you peeking at me when I'm changing!"

The bell rings loud and long.

"Up, up on your feet, get up!" she orders, her hands beating the air. She goes to the door and closes it, and from there, right hand on her heart, she leads all of you with her shrill voice: "I pledge allegiance TO"—the word explodes, a signal for you to hurl your hands, palms upturned, at the flag to one side of her desk—"the flag of the United States of America and to the republic for which it stands, one nation, indivisible, with liberty and justice for all." Then you sing, "My country 'tis of thee, sweet land of liberty . . . " She directs you with great energy, her arms thrashing, her whole person commanding you to sing louder and louder.

Three tardy pupils push open the door and enter. A deep frown stops them, then a left arm reaches out and grabs one of them—the right arm goes on directing—shakes him and pinches him twice before he escapes her grasp.

The singing ends and she turns on the late comers, "Disrupters of ceremony!" The three cringe. "I get here early for your benefit, not mine! Yours! Why can't you do the same! You're not in Mexico! You're in America! We do things on time here! Understand? On time!" She pauses to breathe then continues scolding, "You've abused the privilege of pledging allegiance to the greatest nation in the world. We do it only five times a week! Don't you have any pride? They should send you back where you came from!"

She starts the same way every morning, the heat of her fury unchanged as the school year wears on.

"*Papá*, she makes us pledge allegiance to the flag," you say to your father in Spanish. "She says it's an honor to die for the flag." You look deep into your father's face.

"¡*Mierda*! She's wrong! She shouldn't make children say what they don't understand," he answers you. "Tell me what you say," he demands. He knows the pledge, had to learn it when he became a citizen of the United States, but he wants to test you, wants to see how well you know it.

You learned the pledge in kindergarten and said it every school day the year before, in the first grade. But your teacher did not explain it to you. You and the others said it at the beginning of each school day. Nothing more. You clear your throat and recite: "I pledge allegiance to . . . with liberty and justice for all."

"¡*Pura mierda*! It's not true!" your father protests. "That liberty and justice for all doesn't include Mexicans. They crap on us! They've been dong it since they stole all that land from us—California, Texas, New Mexico . . . "

"I don't understand, *papá*," you say, and you want to

35

understand.

"They don't treat us right, haven't you noticed? We aren't like them, *real* people, as far as they're concerned."

"The flag, *papá*, is it wrong to pledge allegiance to it?"

"The trouble with you Americans," your *papá* answers as he winks at you, "is that you wave your flag and play your national anthem every time you take a shit!" He laughs; you remain silent. "We don't do that in Mexico. We wave the flag and play our national anthem only on special occasions. Not every day. How can those things have any meaning if you do them every day?"

Then he talks to you about the Mexican flag, lovingly, about Hidalgo, Pípila, Juárez, the *niños héroes*, talks to you as no one has ever talked to you about the American flag. He talks to you about Mexico, its beauty, its poverty. He explains to you that for Mexicans, Mexico is the best country in the world, even when they have to leave it.

Once, a stranger asked you, "Boy, what's your nationality?" And you answered, throwing out your chest, "American!" The stranger laughed and said, "Yeah, you're American all right, but with a black Mexican ass!" It made you mad, made you think of what your *güero* playmates say to you when they get angry with you—"Fuckin' Messkin, why don'tcha go back to Mexico where you came from!"

She does not, cannot, know the turmoil she causes in you. At seven you already know you are and are not an American. You were born in Chicago and that makes you an American citizen, but it is not the same as being an *American*. She, your teacher, hurts and confuses you more than anybody else, always saying ugly things about what and who and how you are. In the morning she wraps you and your classmates in the American flag; afterwards she tells Manny and others of you, "I don't know why they let people like you into *our* country. Ugh!" Like the other children of Mexican parents at your school, you learn to write "Mexican" on forms that ask for your nationality. Yet you know you are not Mexican like those born and educated in Mexico. *Real* Mexicans make a distinction between themselves and *pochos* like you; for them, not even your father is a *real* Mexican any more.

A week ago you were working on your penmanship, squeezing the ink pens so hard that your fingers hurt, your fists slowly guiding the wood shafts fitted with steel points across sheets of wide-lined paper. The inkwell lids were open and the pens, dipped after every word, stained middle fingers at the first joint. She walked up and down the rows observing, scolding, correcting, and paused to watch Teresa Vidal, the best writer in the class. Teresa got nervous and dropped her pen, tried to retrieve it and spattered her with black ink. She looked at the ink spots, grabbed Teresa by the hair and pulled her to her feet. Still holding Teresa's hair, she shook her again and again, screaming, "You idiot! Why are *you people* such idiots? Look at my smock! If you were a boy I'd show you something you'd never forget!"

Around school the older boys say she is built. She has big hips and breasts and when she crosses her legs you look furtively at her exposed thigh where it fleshes out into her rump and makes you think of the wonderful haunch of the horse that pulls the milk wagon past school in the morning. In the beginning you think her face is pretty—pronounced chin, large mouth with very white teeth, and a straight nose beneath an expanse of forehead that is cleanly curved. She has very large clear eyes and soft-looking brown hair. Younger and prettier than your kindergarten and first grade teachers, she wears nice clothes, smells of perfume and is always very clean. Whenever they get the least bit soiled, she washes her hands in a small corner sink and then rubs scented cream into them. She is the cleanest person you know.

You know as much about girls as anyone your age. You have learned from older boys and from pictures. You know about their secret. Their secret place—know where it is and what it's for. But you have never seen a real one, only those of babies and animals, especially dogs. Once you touched Margie's, but you couldn't see anything because the basement was dark and you were scared—it was soft and had a deep line in it. *Pussy* is like *puppy* or *bunny*, a soft word, like the young rabbits in the park, frightened and always trying to hide; like the pussy willows you love to touch with your fingertips. After a time you do not think of her pussy or any other part of her. But in the beginning you wished you could go into the cloakroom when she was changing, smell her there in the dark, lift her skirt and breathe her sweetness and see what she guards from you so carefully, see the hair the older boys say she has there, beautiful like the hair on her head, soft and brown.

Nobody misbehaves in her class. She closes her door to laughter and happiness and nobody defies her. And nobody whispers in her class. She teaches you fear, makes you nervous, confuses you, and when she scolds you she makes you lose your self-control, which makes her furious. On her desk she keeps two wood pointers, yard-long spears that taper into bullet-shaped tips of black rubber. They are there for emergencies, to throw at anyone who forgets where he is, above all at sassers—she can't stand a single word of back talk. She keeps them there for Manuel Campos and Mario López and Frederick Douglass Snead and Ernest Krause and Yonko Babich, who howl at the top of their voice when she so much as touches them. With the pointers she keeps their voices down.

Mrs. Bolen's class is next door. She teaches vocational arts and her pupils are the biggest, toughest boys in school—delinquents or near-delinquents who refuse to study but are forced to attend school. The print shop is their classroom and Mrs. Bolen gets them to do beautiful work with the old equipment and machinery. Her boys call her Mom and everybody calls them Mom Bolen's boys. One afternoon Mom is called away and she distributes her boys among the other teachers.

The worst boy is sent to your class. He throws open the door and explains as he walks in, "Mom hadda go somewheres. She told me to come here." He scowls and taps his feet impatiently.

"Mrs. Bolen had to go somewhere, not Mom!" she corrects.

"That's what I said, she hadda go somewheres," he growls.

"Sit back there, dummy!" she shouts, pointing to an empty desk at the back of the class. "And I don't want any trouble from you, just sit there and shut up! I'm not Mrs. Bolen and I won't fool with you! You should have brought a book."

He looks at her, pulls a comic book from his pocket, walks to the back of the class and sits down. His body is too big for the little desk and he squirms, his legs thrash, he mumbles to himself and talks to those around him. They try to ignore him but he keeps at them.

"I told you to shut up," she threatens, "now shut up!"

"Shuddup yourself!" he challenges.

She grabs one of her spears and throws it at the trouble maker. He ducks—and those around him do too—and the spear crashes against the wall. Silent and unbelieving, all of you watch. He leaps from his seat and picks up the spear as she reaches for the second one. He wings it at her; she dodges it. It bangs into the corner behind her and his words explode in the air, "Stick it up your ass!"

She springs from behind her desk, swinging the spear like a sword, chasing him. He darts into the cloakroom, through it and the doors before she can catch him. She turns to face all of you and finds your eyes fixed on her. She screams, "Get back to work, you busy bodies!" She shakes the weapon at you and threatens, "Or I'll give you some of this! Who said you could watch? Why didn't somebody trip him if you're so interested?" Then she brings the pointer crashing down on one desk after another, just missing arms, hands, heads.

Slowly, weeks and months pass by and it seems to you and your classmates that you spend more time watching her from the corner of your eye than you do on school work. You do only one thing that everybody—including her—enjoys. You don't know why she does it, don't know if it's a game. Suddenly she tells you to stop what you're doing, and then she gives you words and tells you to give her words that rhyme with the ones she gives you.

"Run," she starts.

You respond with, "Fun, bun, sun, gun, ton, done, none, one." And finding the rhythm, knowing, without having to be told, that she wants one-syllable words, the most daring of you invent them: "pun, shun, kun," and then others take courage and join in: "chun, blun, hun, scun, mun," until you exhaust the rhyme and she moves on to another word. She never interrupts you. Sometimes she smiles, sometimes laughs.

"Stumble," she continues.

You offer, "Bumble, crumble, tumble, grumble, mumble, jumble, fumble, humble," and then, "dumble, kumble, lumble, wumble, chumble, drumble, trumble."

Once she says, "Kiss."

The words come fast, "Miss, sis, this, hiss, Chris, bliss," and you say, "piss," realizing too late what you have said. You cringe and await the inevitable, but it does not come. She says nothing and moves on to the next word, but you never again take part in her word-rhyming exercise.

Her favorites are her cloakroom guards and two or three other girls. They are like puppets when she needs them.

40

Some of you say she hates boys. But there are girls, Teresa Vidal for example, who say she is like those aunts and uncles who prefer some nieces and nephews to others. There are even parents like that. She is moody and you find safety in being as watchful and silent as you can. You do not tell your parents about her because they believe your teachers outdo themselves for you. She is there always, never sick, always there.

In time you learn things about her personal life. She brings pictures to school, holds them at arm's length to look at them, smiles, laughs, spreads them across her desk, does everything possible to attract your attention to what she is doing. When she tires of looking alone she calls her girls to join her: "Dorothy, Ann, Margaret, come up here. I want to show you something. The rest of you go on working. Don't let me catch you looking up here!" She shares nothing with you.

She has two children, girls six and eight. Her husband is good-looking. All wear nice clothes. Her house is beautiful; only they live in it. There are pictures of her back yard, of birthday parties, her church, the zoo, museums . . .

The second year is coming to an end and you have all these things to remember.

What you will remember more than anything else is what she does to Manuel Campos in the final week. Manny is the toughest boy in the class, and the dirtiest. His pants are dirty and torn and so is his shirt and you can see the safety pins that hold them together. He wears the same clothes day after day and every morning she orders him to wash his face and hands in the low sink in the hallway where the janitor washes his mops. He doesn't wear socks and his shoes are full of holes and so scuffed that they're gray. On his feet you can see *costras*, crusts of dirt. He never combs his hair. That's how Manny is and all of you know it and all of you accept it. Manny is smart and, whatever she thinks, he doesn't make trouble in class. But outside he doesn't take anything from anybody and fights a lot because the older boys make fun of his clothes and the way he sometimes smells.

Something Manny does—you don't know what, never will— suddenly makes her roar, pounce on him, grab him by the hair and drag him to the front of the class. She slaps him and he doesn't even try to protect himself. She makes him stand there and tells all of you to punch him in the face and says that she'll punch anyone who refuses. You line up along the side wall and across the back of the room, all of you, boys and girls, and start punching him. He is your best friend because he protects you on the playground. When it's your turn she is washing her hands in her little sink and she doesn't see everything. You stand before Manny and tears rush to your eyes. Manny's mouth and nose are bleeding; his lips and face are swollen. He looks right into your eyes and without saying a word orders you to punch him, you will still be friends. You ball up your hand and punch him. Through the whole thing Manny doesn't cry out or flinch.

When it's all over she drags him down the hall to the janitor's low sink where she makes him wash his face with the strong brown bar of American Family soap.

The Birthday Present

Morning. Softly, your mother calls you, "Amado, Amado," touches you gently and you open your eyes, nod to her. Without waking your brothers you slip out of the big bed, pull on your socks, pants, and sit on the floor to put your shoes on. The thought that you will be ten years old next week is increasingly with you as your birthday approaches. Taking soap and a towel from the kitchen, you step into the dim hallway and make your way to the toilet shared with two other families. Good, you think, there's no one here. A tug at the cord fills the little room with light and a mouse darts out, thin and gray. You shudder and close the door. A single long hair in the sink makes your flesh crawl; you turn on the faucet full force and water plunges into the bowl, engulfs the hair and swirls it down the drain. Cold water on your face, soap, your hands work up a lather. You rinse. As you dry yourself you are thinking that you'll be ten next week, not nine anymore, two numbers. Maybe the time will go faster after that. You do not want to be a boy longer than you have to.

Back in the flat you sit at the kitchen table while your mother bends over the stove, her back to you. "*Sólo avena, mamá*, just oatmeal," you say. She is scarcely taller than you, but now as you look at her she appears smaller to you, her narrow shoulders narrower than you remember. She turns and moves toward you with a bowl and a spoon, sets them down in front of you, and you look into her eyes and smile. She strokes your hair.

Of the children, you, Amado, are the light sleeper. Even before you went to kindergarten, you would get up at the first sounds of her stirring in the kitchen. You like to get ready without hurrying, want to have time to see things on your way

43

to school, a walk of almost five blocks, to have time to stop if you want to. Ramiro, your brother, runs all the way because he can't get up on time—as if someone brushed him with glue at night, causing him to thrash about in the morning, trying to free himself from the bed.

Notebook in hand, you hug your mother and kiss her. Then she pours you a tablespoon of cod-liver oil and you gulp it down, pucker, open your mouth, and she places a sliver of *canela*, cinnamon, on your tongue. An orange would be better, you think, and start down the stairs, nibbling like a rodent. You smile— she never kisses you right after you take the oil. You pull open the door and enter the street.

Cars turning at 85th Street, following the winding way that takes them north to Russell Square Park, past St. Michael's, beyond the steel mills. The white milk wagon, its big spoked wheels turning with a hard sound that cuts through the hollow clomp-clomp, clomp-clomp of the horse that goes along with blinders, strong and graceful. Women coming from stores, brown bags cradled in their arms. Men walking listlessly, hands deep in their pockets. People at corners waiting for streeetcars. You make your way down the street. More women, sweeping front porches, narrow door stoops. Jobbers and deliverymen at stores and taverns. Other children going to school.

You continue south, spy the tall gates at the railroad crossing and then stop to watch a man painting window frames white on the other side of the street. Your eyes take in the surrounding buildings—peeling paint, blackened exteriors, cracked windows. A streetcar goes by. You turn and look north, up the long corridor of streets, streets without trees. You move on. At the crossing the red streetcar fails to slow down and the trolley jumps from the powerline, flexing back and forth as the streetcar comes to a halt on the railroad tracks. The conductor opens the back window, pulls the trolley line and the trolley arcs back. Now its tip reaches up, swaying slightly, until the sheave makes contact with the powerline. The streetcar lurches forward.

You reach the crossing, the gates are up, black and white like a zebra, you look to your left. The train yard, an engine pulling gondolas full of coke. You pause, you stop. Just beyond you the engine slams to a halt, suddenly, and a tremor shudders through the cars, shakes coke loose. A man throws a switch, waves, the engine starts up slowly. In the background, steel mills, blue sky above. You walk on, turn your head to the right. A big brick roundhouse, a network of railroad tracks in the vast yard that disappears behind the row of houses. The tracks behind you now. On your left, abruptly, the high wooden fence, dull brown, words and names knifed into it, white chalk, yellow. Across the street a cyclone fence, lines of boxcars everywhere. Your mind jumps forward, swiftly, following the brown fence, turns left for a block, turns right, and then straight ahead, fence and more fence, moving left whenever it can, east, to the lake. Before you reach the corner you are back. The dangerous crossing.

Standing on the corner you wait for a chance to cross; cars sweeping around the wide curve. No patrol boy yet. There she comes in her car, Mrs. Flynn. You smile and wave at your teacher. She takes the curve, you smiling and waving still, but she does not wave, does not turn to look at you. You run across the street, into the alley where the street would go if it didn't make the wide turn. It is your shortcut to the school's door, you walk very slowly. Now you concentrate, your neck rigid, draw back your lips, a narrow opening between them, try to fold your tongue and draw it back a little, right at the center of its front edge, try to form the right opening at the very center of your mouth, tongue and lips fused because it's all in the right coming together of tongue and lips. You blow through the opening gently at first and then with force and nothing happens. How does he do it, you ask yourself. For months you have been trying to do it, to whistle in that loud, shrill way that makes someone two blocks away turn around. Like your father.

Hanging on a clothesline, something new, you see it—a black metal cage. Inside, a bright green parrot. A good birthday present! Teach it to whistle. You smile. Piles of garbage on either side of you, rats scurry at your approach. At the base of the tree, a raccoon on a long chain. It sees you and climbs the tree. And then a Coca Cola bottle, two cents, and you hurry toward it, but it's broken. You kick it. Out of the alley, you cross the street, go toward the other children. Minutes later the first bell rings.

In the morning the gym class meets on the school playground. Yonko Babich and Manuel Campos are in charge. Manny tosses the bat to Yonko, high, vertically. Yonko catches it at the fat end with one hand. They work their hands up the bat taking turns and the last full hand on the bat wins, chooses first. Quickly the teams are picked—Manny and Yonko calling out names—best players first.

"Hey Yonko, you take Amado. We haddum the last time," Manny explains.

"Bull! He's yours! It's your turn to choose an' he's the only one left." Yonko turns to you, "You're with them, Fuentes, go on." And to Manny, "Unless you want Fuentes to ump."

"No! Everyone's gotta play, you know that! You heard what the teacher said, everyone. No umps."

"He's yours! I take Fuentes only when I have to!"

You feel like two people, both undesirable. You're one of the smallest boys in the group. But it isn't that, you know it. It's that softball requires skills that you don't have—catching, throwing, hitting, running bases. You remember that time when you were on Yonko's team, you made seven errors in right field when Manny ordered everyone to bat lefthanded. Yonko kept shouting, "You shithead! You shithead!"

"Okay, we'll take 'um! Come on Amado! But don't ask

me for no goddamn favors, Yonko! He's a damn good swimmer! Best swimmer here!"

"I give a shit! We're playin' baseball, not goin' swimmin'! Let 'um go swimmin' if he wants to."

You feel angry and humiliated. You don't want to play,
but you have to. If you had those two in the water, you'd
drown them, they swim like babies, worse!

After the game they put their softball feelings about you
aside. You know that when you're a man you won't have to
play baseball. But that's a long way off.

One day is like another, long and endless. You want your
birthday to come and go, your life to rush forward. For about
a year now you've held a job. You have "responsibilities."
More than ever you feel distant from your schoolmates. After
school, and in the summer, all they do is play. Why shouldn't
they be good ball players! To feel older than you do is what
you want, older than you feel with your body like a seven-
year-old's. You want to *be* older.

Whenever you see a newsboy you remember you used to
sell newspapers. It was wanting things, needing money, that
made you look for a job and you ended up with those Mexican papers: *El ABC*, *El Anunciador*. You sold *El Anunciador*
for a penny—"One for me and one for you, *muchacho*," the
printer told you when you picked up the papers. *El ABC* was
three cents, harder to sell, with news about Mexico, not like
El Anunciador with only barrio news. One cent for you and
two for the man who delivered the papers to you and you had
to return what you didn't sell or pay two cents for each one.
You made the rounds with both papers and learned how to sell
them, where to sell them, learned to talk with adults, reached
out little by little until you covered the whole community. You

had regular customers who bought both papers and sometimes owed you money. Nobody paid in advance. On Saturdays and Sundays you were busy from morning until evening, careful always with your money, careful to avoid older boys who might take it from you. You hated that job—too much work and too little pay and always alone.

Then you found another job. At Pito Loco's barber shop, one of your best paper stops. Pito bought two of each for his customers to read, and sometimes customers bought papers to take home. When you first thought of asking Pito Loco for a job, the barber shop had been your stop for two months. It needed a good cleaning, someone with a new eye who would keep it clean. You spoke to him in Spanish.

"Don Pito, I'm looking for a different job. *Por favor*, give me a job, you won't be sorry. *Soy muy trabajador*, I'm a good worker. Try me out for a while."

Pito looked at you blankly for a moment and then smiled. "*Sí, flaco*, skinny," he said, "you can start Monday. But I don't need a *huevón*, if you're a *huevón* I won't pay you. *Aquí te chingas*, you'll bust your balls here, *te lo prometo*, I promise you. I'll pay you fifty cents a week and you can keep anything you find on the floor." You agreed and after that weekend you gave up the papers.

And Pito Loco has kept his promise. Through the week you get to the barber shop at seven in the evening. Closing time is eight but mostly the shop is open until ten. On Saturdays you work from noon until closing and help Pito's wife clean their flat. On Sundays the shop is closed. It's where Pito and his musician friends gather to make music. He plays the saxophone— that's why they call him *Pito Loco*. Ashtrays, mirrors, sinks, cabinets, floor, you keep these clean and shining. The black hair, like yours, you sweep up and empty into a steel drum that stands in a corner. Sometimes you find money on the floor. It's yours to keep. Once a week you struggle with the drum through the back door and wrestle it into the alley. You run errands for Pito and customers; some of the customers tip you. The floor—there are men spit on it—you mop last. Your duties grow with time and after months he pays you a dollar a week. In the shop you move among men who do not treat you like a child—they behave as if you were another adult. You are more at ease with them than you are with your baseball- and football- and basketball-playing schoolmates.

When you look back now on what happened, you see that there was no way of avoiding it. It happened and neither you nor your mother knew it would. She borrowed money from you and promised to pay it back as soon as she could, borrowed again the following week and again the week after that and then the two of you realized she could never pay you back. She wept with embarrassment and you told her it didn't matter. You knew what she bought with the money—sometimes it was milk, soup bones, tripe, flour for the tortillas she made daily; sometimes it was lard, rice, beans, and because you like it, bread.

You know your mother counts on you. You discovered it when she became indebted to you so that the family might have a little more. You feel angry and cheated because you can't buy what you want with your own money, and only the thought of your mother, her selflessness, makes it possible for you to bear the injustice. But there are moments when you hate her for having started all this, for having asked you. Before you worked, the family got along somehow on what your father made working in the mill two or three days a week. Still, you have a little money left after meeting your "responsibilities"—enough for a candy bar every now and then, for a bottle of pop, a movie, a hot-dog.

If you could have anything you wanted for this birthday, you would ask for a man's body. Your own embarrasses you when you play with boys your age. In the water you're safe, your body submerged, out of view. Sometimes you wish you were a fish, and the only school in your life the company of other fishes. It is the gym class that you dislike, especially when it meets outside for team sports.

You are an average student, but you like to read, you like it a lot—when you sold newspapers you used to read them from beginning to end—and you like school, you like to be close to classmates who do their lessons beside you. It's good to see them next to you, feels good to have them there after the many hours you spend with adults. In the classroom you have a habit of suddenly looking around at your classmates and smiling at them, as if they were yours, your brothers and sisters. It is a broad smile that shows your teeth and draws your teacher's attention— Mrs. Flynn.

She points a finger at you, shouts, scolding you: "Whatever you're doing, Um-mah-dough, cut it out this instant! And wipe that stupid smile from your face or I'll wipe it off for you!" You shrink as several heads turn to look at you. Your smile has brought you trouble before; you must control it.

Mrs. Flynn. When she isn't watching you, you observe her stealthily, once, twice, again. Seated at her desk. Long head, graying hair, hollows at her temples, high cheekbones above sunken cheeks. A nose like a knife blade, her mouth a slit, chin hard and square, its skin red and flaky. Lean. Sharp bones at the collar and shoulders, long arms, the breastbone high and stony. She watches you and the others with cold unsmiling eyes that sharpen to fishhooks when she spots "a troublemaker." When she passes out paper, paste, chalk, crayons, she does it with a frown, her eyes and fingers checking and rechecking to make sure she hands out no more than she must. She tries always to keep a certain distance from you and the others, and she sniffs constantly when she has to be near you. She tells you to have your mothers mend your clothes, to have them wash your clothes just as soon as they start to give off "those awful body smells."

You want her to like you—you want everybody to like you at all times. But especially her because she's so important to you. You have been squirreling money away for months to buy yourself a birthday present. Something that you know will please her too. The days crawl by.

The night before your birthday you go to bed thinking of the following day. Ten years old at last! For a moment you give in to wishing, you think of roller-skates, the kind with good bearings and red wheels that hum when they're spinning. If you had them you would skate to school every day. You think of a bike, you think of swim fins, you think . . . Your head fills with visions, feels light, and then gradually grows heavy and finally you fall asleep.

You are swimming underwater, a small happy fish. Above you, you see fishhooks and know they are Yonko's and Manny's. You swim around the fishhooks. Suddenly you feel an explosion inside you and discover that you have arms and legs. A frog! Your limbs grow, long legs tapering down to ankles that flare out into black fins, arms ending in huge webbed hands like baseball mitts. You have been underwater too long and thrash your way up, careful to avoid not two, but a tangle of hooks now. You burst through the surface and find yourself in a vast field. There, you smile and run, sunshine raining down on you as you nimbly pluck rainbow-feathered birds from the sky, your long-fingered hands stroking and releasing them, your arms fluid and marvelous in their movement.

Morning. You enter the kitchen for breakfast. Your mother turns to look at you and her eyes go wide with surprise and approval. You are wearing new pants and a new shirt, both the dark blue color of a Cub Scout uniform. "*Feliz cumpleaños*, happy birthday!" she greets you. She moves toward you, hugs and kisses you.

A faint smile touches your face. "*Le gustan*, you like them?" you ask. "I've been saving for a long time," you add.

"*Sí, Sí*," she answers, "you look so handsome, *guapo*."

The aromas in the kitchen make you suddenly hungry and you sit at the table. The others are still asleep. She serves you a glass of milk, a big chocolate-covered doughnut, a dish of rice pudding. A smile springs to your face and you dunk the doughnut in the milk. Then you eat the rice pudding, savoring the raisins and the coarsely ground cinnamon. At the door she takes you into her arms and tells you that you can skip the cod-liver oil.

Mrs. Flynn enters the classroom and drops her things on the desk. She glares. Shifting in your seats, you and the others exchange nervous glances. After the bell rings she leads you through the pledge to the flag. Her voice is shrill, several tones higher than normal. Except for the redness at her chin, her face is a porcelain mask, pale and brittle and crazed in a fine network of tiny blue vessels. She begins to take attendance, pronouncing each name slowly, pausing to judge and predict. In deepest silence, you and the others listen, a silence so deep that her voice echoes in it.

"Mah-ree-ah Alvarez. You dirty little thing! I'll bet you use water only for drinking. You'll be somebody's maid when you grow up and then you'll learn about soap . . . Hoe-zay Castañeda. You stinky devil! When was the last time you took a bath? A garbage man, that's what you'll be, a garbage man! What else are you good for? . . . Joan Cole. You've been around these others too long! You're starting to look like them. A shame you have such blue eyes! . . . Ray-mown

Cortez. Always clean, but dumb. So what good does it do you? You'll never make it out of this God forsaken neighborhood . . . Curtis Davis. Curtis can give most of you a lesson. He's colored, but he's scrubbed and polite. Even Curtis is better than most of you! Make a fine janitor right here in this school . . . Cone-cep-see-OHN Escobar. That's a stupid name! What's the matter with your parents? How can you do anything with a name like that? . . . Um-mah-dough Foo-en-tehs. You idiot! Always smiling like a half-wit and when I call on you you don't say anything! You'll wind up in the steel mill like your father and you deserve it!" She says something to all of you, stuns you with her bluntness.

In spite of her words, you want her to notice your new clothes. You want her to say something about them, as several classmates have. You are wearing them for her as much as for yourself. But she says nothing more about you. She hands out the spelling books and all of you start the lesson, bent over your desks. You drive away all thought of her and your clothes and concentrate on the new words.

After a few minutes your mind strays, you remember your new clothes and your hand drops to your lap. You move your hand along your fly, back and forth along its length, back and forth, and now your fingers pause at each button. You smile. You are thinking of your other pants—hand-me-downs, their frayed flies held fast with safety-pins. Again you run your fingers along the fly, half expecting to touch metal, and again you smile. You look up and the fishhooks in Mrs. Flynn's eyes dig into you. She has been watching you. You struggle to stifle the smile, you blush, lower your head.

Suddenly she springs and rushes at you, grabs you by the hair and drags you into the hall before you can raise a terrified hand to protect yourself. With a powerful jerk she lifts you to your feet and her bony hand strikes you twice—sharp, stinging blows that mark your face. "You filthy little bastard!" she spits at you, "If I ever catch you doing that again I'll break your neck."

When the bell rings you race out of the building, across the street and into the alley. She has reached a part of you not even Yonko and Manny have touched. You walk along slowly, tears scalding your cheeks. Automatically your lips and tongue begin to shape the platform from which you hope to launch the sound. You blow gently and a soft, high-pitched whistle moves through the air. You stiffen. Then you blow harder and the air around you vibrates with the shrillness of the sound. Now you stop and fill your lungs and blow with all your might and the note, like a shriek, knifes forward, rending the air with desperation and rage.

Killdeer

They went in April when the weather had warmed. Sometimes it was early in April, sometimes late, but it was always in April. They went to clear and hoe the land, to get it ready for planting, and to get a jump on the others. This year would be no different. He, with their help, would try to finish first. He liked it that way—being first, in everything, always. They knew he was that way, was happy that way, and they had learned to bend to his happiness and his other feelings too.

He had an old bike that looked new, had bought it piece by piece—frame here, fork there, sprocket wheel and chain in this place, pedals and handlebars in that, wheels and saddle in another—until he had all the parts he needed to put it together, cleaned them of rust and grime, assembled it and painted it so well that it looked like a new black bike. In April, when it got warm, he mounted the bike and rode out to his *milpa* at the edge of the city. It was just beyond the paved street, off a dirt road that cut through the land. He left the bike at the edge of the *milpa* and wandered through it looking at the soil and kicking it here, poking it there, digging his hands into it in other places. Satisfied with what he saw, he got on his bike and left.

"*Ahora sí*, it's time now. You'll go with me on Saturday," he said when they returned from school, his voice firm with resolve. He spoke Spanish to them—clear, full syllables—always had. When they began to reject it under pressure from teachers and classmates who knew only one language, he forbade them to speak English in his presence.

The two accepted his words calmly. The waiting, which had begun in March when they went into the streets in search of manure for the bedding plants, was now over. Lázaro winked at Jaime, his younger brother.

On Saturday, in the early morning, Jaime came down the back stairs, carrying the food his mother had packed; his brother and father followed, each with a gallon jug of water. They crossed the back yard to the padlocked coal shed where the wagon and tools were kept. Tools, food, water, rope, sacks and newspapers went into the wagon and then José María pulled it out to the alley. He had built it years before, a man's wagon—a large wooden bed on steel axletrees fitted with heavy iron wheels, the wooden sides detachable. It served José María well, at times seemed an extension of the man, and he cared for it—cleaning and greasing the axles regularly, keeping its wooden cage solid, the nuts always oiled and tight on the sturdy bolts—as he might have cared for his body if it had turned on axles and been held fast by nuts and bolts. Lázaro could remember when his father built it, yet he had the impression that it had been with them always. He and his brothers had grown up with it, and he and Jaime still played in it, sometimes in the darkness of the shed, sometimes in the back yard, where they built it up with planks into a small house on wheels, its tarp a roof billowing gently with the wind. Jaime could not look at it without remembering it had once withstood a terrible storm with them. It had been bigger then, he, much smaller.

"*Ya, vámonos.*" He gave the order over his shoulder, his back to them as he slipped the door's hook into the eye in the post. Lázaro took up the handle and pulled; Jaime pushed from behind. The wheels turned slowly, gathered speed, and then rolled as easily as the boys walked. José María followed behind them, pushing his bicycle. Once out of the alley, at 86th Street, they took to the street and he mounted his bike and rode off. Without running, they went as fast as they could, knowing he would be waiting for them when they got there. He had an enormous capacity for work.

He always took the fastest route, going southwest and

avoiding traffic. Lázaro and Jaime sometimes followed unfamiliar streets. But all their routes, like his, led them to Torrence Avenue and 95th Street. From there, acres of land with few trees reached south as far as the 103rd Street bridge and west to the highway—railroad land fallen into disuse. It hid old wells and scant remains of structures razed long ago. Their *milpa* was off Torrence Avenue, just west of where the long curve ended. José María, like other Mexican immigrants, had found his way there some years earlier, had cleared several acres, turned them over with a hoe and worked the simple magic that gave him corn, tomatoes, potatoes, squash, coriander and much more. It was more land and richer than any his father had cultivated in Mexico. He took it, worked it and felt like a landowner.

It was still chilly when Lázaro and Jaime got to Torrence Avenue. The damp air was dense with green aromas and a growing medley of sounds. They stopped at their *milpa*, a rectangular tract flanked by a road and stretching perpendicularly from Torrence Avenue to where José María had built a shack some years before. With his sons, José María had cleared the land of weeds and grass so thick and tough that he would have abandoned the undertaking had the land not been easy to reach and close to water—a fire hydrant on a small street just off Torrence. Above, the sky was cloudless and a strong sun was beginning to deepen the blue. He stepped out of the *milpa* and came to meet them.

"We'll start there, *allí*," he said and pointed. They brought the wagon alongside the shack and he saw drops of moisture glisten on the spokes of the wheels. The tracks in the dew-soaked grass were dark in the bright sun, prints in the green pile of the earth's velvet. The bike was against the shack, out of the way.

"Lázaro, the water, I want it cooled," he called out as he opened the door to the shack. Sunlight poured in, washing cobwebs in corners and along edges.

The boy nodded, reached into the wagon and took a length of rope and one of jugs of water. Jaime took the other and followed his brother to the old well behind the shack. There was never much water in it, three or four feet, but it stayed cold, if they kept the well covered. It served as their cooler. If they drew the water from it, it took hours to fill again. Lázaro pushed one end of the rope through the glass ear and tied it; with the other end he did the same to the second jug. Then he lowered them one at a time, tied the rope to a two-by-four and laid it across the rim of the well.

José María unlatched the hinged wooden squares that sealed the windows, swung them back and a torrent of light rushed in. He took off his jacket and hung it on a nail; the flannel shirt he was wearing would be enough to keep him warm once he started working. Now the boys removed their jackets. They wore sweaters over thin cotton shirts.

He went to the wagon, took his hoe and ran his hands back and forth along the length of the handle, removing half a year's dust. "Ready to work?" he asked. "I want everything cleared away. Rake it into piles. Understand?"

"*Sí, papá*," Lázaro answered.

José María reached into his back pocket for a triangular file, took the big mortar hoe in his left hand, just behind the blade, and began to sharpen the cutting edge. Across years José María's hands had worn smooth the upper half of the hoe's shaft and it shone in the sun, even as the thick skin on the palms of his hands would shine after working with the tool for a while, and the hard calluses would begin to look like the dense polished knots in the wood.

The boys went to what had been a corn field, Jaime to one edge, Lázaro to the other. It was a field of broken stalks, the result of the autumn trampling that had followed the final harvest. Dry stumps clung to the soil with radiating roots, and here and there stood withered spears, stalks that some-how had straightened themselves after the trampling. They gathered these remains, heaping them in mounds, working ever closer to each other until they met in the center of the field.

"It's gonna get hot," Lázaro remarked, dropping an armload of stalks on the ground.

"Feels like May," Jaime said, dumping his armful on the pile. "How long do you think we'll be here?" he asked.

"All day if the weather stays like this. We'll get back just before dark."

José María's task was simple—to turn over the earth for planting. The cleanest strip of his *milpa* was where the potatoes had been; he started there. He did not use a spade, did not like it—all that moving around, bending over and moving backward. The hoe was faster. With it he went forward at a pace he could hold all day. He hoed right-handed and left-handed, switching over without losing a stroke, controlling perfectly the cut he made, slicing the earth thin when it was dense and unyielding, thick when it gave way easily, the left corner of the blade entering first when it fell from the left, the right corner first when it fell from the right. He moved with a constant rhythm, the hoe starting its swing at his feet, rising in a curve above his head, pausing just long enough to reverse its direction and then falling in a swift arc at his feet. It swung with the exactness of a pendulum, sometimes revolving a half turn, the back of the blade hammering a hard clump and smashing it.

José María paused to observe his sons. They would grow up one day and the thought of their working in the steel mill tormented him. He slashed the earth but could not still his foreman's voice—"Your sons will work for me too, Hoezay, you'll see." He slashed harder, faster, angry with his foreman, and himself for having brought his sons to a life of possible entrapment in the mill.

Now Lázaro called out to him—the stalks were ready for burning. José María waved. He put down his hoe, walked to the wagon, took some paper and went toward the boys. "Go on with the rest. *Allí*," he said, pointing to the remains of tomato plants. He lit the fires himself, going from heap to heap. Years before, one of his older sons at play had set fire to the porch of the house where they lived.

When they reached the wagon they removed their sweaters and took up their rakes. Jaime's had a shorter handle and a smaller head, but it was heavier than the other. It was unfair, Jaime thought, that his father should have given him the hoe just because it was smaller, but he did not complain.

"Let's take a drink," Lázaro invited.

"Okay," Jaime accepted.

Lázaro pulled up the cold jug. Jaime, off to one side, spread his legs and fired a stream at a big green fly on a rock just beyond him. He missed, overshooting the mark. "Shit!" he muttered and trained the jet down. He shook it off, put it back into his pants and saw the drops on his shoes. Lázaro handed him the jug and left. Jaime was still drinking when he heard the whistle and turned to see his father put his hand up to his mouth, tilt his head back and raise his elbow. Jaime waved, freed the jug and took it to him.

José María, legs spread, had his back to him. Jaime heard the heavy splash, saw the dark stain spread on the ground. Without moving his feet, the man turned to see where the boy was and the boy saw it in his hand—thick as the hoe handle, the head large and ruddy. Jaime smiled, wondered if his would be like that some day, hoped it would be bigger. The splashing stopped. José María turned around, reached for the jug, raised and tipped it, taking long drafts. His "Ahh" told Jaime he had finished. "Be careful putting it back," José María warned, handing the jug to the boy.

There was little left of last year's thick, green tomato plants. They had shriveled almost to nothing—dark, withered branches like stiff, dirty henequen twine—still rooted in places. Quickly, with their rakes, the boys heaped the stuff.

The air was heavy with the smell of cornstalks that had flamed fast and now smoldered, a mildly pungent smell laced with a sweetness the burning had released.

"They're having free movies at the YMCA," Jaime said, slamming his rake to the ground. They had finished.

"I don't like them Y movies. All that stuff about nature and travel. Makes you feel bad jus' to see them places when you know you ain't never going there," Lázaro complained. They walked toward the wagon.

"But it's jus' like being there!" Jaime pointed out. A meadowlark flew overhead and his eyes followed it.

"Shit! I don't like 'em!" Lázaro said with finality.

They stood the rakes against the wagon and took their hoes. Lázaro looked out to where his father was and saw all he had done. The earth was darker where it had been hoed. He watched his father swing the long-handled tool up down up down, like a pendulum turned on its side. The sun was hot now and a film of perspiration covered the boy's forehead.

"It'd be nice now coolin' off in the Y pool," Jaime said wistfully. He pulled up the jug and took a long drink.

"Why d'you think of that stuff when you know we gotta be here?" Lázaro asked, holding out his hands for the jug.

"'Cause I'd rather be there than here."

Side by side three hoes now plowed the earth.

At noon José María burned the other piles and then called his sons to eat. From a corner of the shack he took a pail, rope inside, went to the well and drew. He rinsed his hands and face in the cold water and dried himself with a piece of terrycloth. The boys took their turn rinsing and Lázaro emptied the pail.

At the edge of the *milpa* José María started a fire in the tin stove he had made from a five-gallon can. Beside it, on a wooden crate, he placed salt, a jar of pickled *jalapeños*, and slices of a dark, coarsely textured bread sugared with *piloncillo*. Then he opened a box that had been carefully packed and took out the tacos. There were several kinds—*frijoles refritos*, potatoes and eggs, rice and tomatoes, pork in a thick red sauce—all made with flour tortillas. They were still warm. He took the tacos they wanted and put them on the stove and the heat burned off the moisture that had made them too soft. Now they were hot.

Lázaro brought a jug of water and Jaime spread sacks on a hoed spot he had smoothed with his rake. It would be softer there than on the grass, not damp. All was ready.

Long ago he had taught them that if they chewed carefully and ate slowly their hunger would be satisfied. Father and sons ate deliberately, savoring each bite. They were in no hurry to finish. Lázaro took a pinch of salt and sprinkled it evenly across his taco, plunged two fingers into the jar, brought up two slices of *jalapeño* and placed them lengthwise in the bean-filled tortilla. He took a bite and rolled his eyes. José María laughed and roughed the boy's hair. Jaime cradled his egg-and-potato taco on the heel of his hand, seeming to talk to it each time he bit it. José María was eating a pork taco. They bit firmly, cleanly, never taking more than they could chew. And they chewed with their mouth closed, an easy unhurried motion that started at the chin and rolled gracefully up in waves that spent themselves at their temples.

"Good, aren't they?" he said. It was more comment than question and the boys scarcely nodded.

Index fingers and thumbs rescued grains of rice, potatoes, other bits of food. The three sucked fingers and licked palms. They had drunk before eating and now drank sparingly, not wanting to wash away the taste of what they had eaten.

The stove was left to cool, the jug was returned to the well, the remaining food, wrapped and returned to the wagon.

"Tired?" he asked gruffly, holding back a smile.

They did not look at him. "No," Lázaro answered softly. Jaime shook his head.

He laughed with abandon, put an arm around each, drew them to him and lifted them and they laughed too, pleased at his joke. "We'll take a nap," he said, putting them down.

He took four sacks, found a spot in the shallow ditch that surrounded his *milpa*, spread them there and then rolled two others into the pillow. Lázaro and Jaime followed his example. Each spread two sacks in the ditch and used a sweater for a pillow. José María at once fell asleep and in a while Lázaro did too. Jaime lay there with his eyes open.

Resting on his side he looked out across the field—the earth had grown. He could not see as much as when he stood, but what he saw was enormous, more solid than before. He rolled onto his back. The sky was higher now and there was more of it and he felt it pressing down on him. Slender columns of white smoke rose in slow motion, blued gradually and disappeared, their aroma suspended in the air. Again he turned on his side, his face next to the ground, and smelled the earth—he thought of wet unglazed flowerpots. He dug his fingers into the soil and brought up a warm fistful. He dug deeper and this time it was cool. He cupped his hand to his nose, breathing deep and repeatedly. Then he became aware of noises around him and listened attentively. From far off came the faint sound of human voices; he wondered whose they were. A train whistled and freight cars rumbled. He recognized the hum of tires on pavement. The buzz of a distant airplane reached him. Other sounds, muffled and undefined, he could not make out. Now he heard a meadowlark—three clear descending notes, up on the fourth, and again the descent, this time in a single slurred note. It was his favorite birdsong, sweet and crisp and easy to whistle. It seemed to say so much--"run away from here," "you should be at home," "throw your hoe away," "it's for your own good," "learn to be a man," "do the best you can . . . " Was it the one he had seen earlier? There were no meadowlarks in the city. His hand dug into the earth, found the coolness, rested, and he fell asleep.

That afternoon they worked as hard as they had in the morning. At twilight, their food gone, they prepared to leave. The wagon, its sides detached, was turned on its flank to get it into the shack, where they locked it up with the other things. At Torrence Avenue José María mounted his bike, waved and rode off. Lázaro and Jaime went home on foot.

He was eating when they arrived and by the time they finished supper he had bathed and gone to bed. Jaime and his mother talked while Lázaro took a bath. They spoke in Spanish, for she knew little English and pronounced it with an accent that embarrassed her.

"Mamá, tell him to let me go to the movies," he pleaded.

"You know how he is about these things," she said.

"Tell him it'll be just this once," he begged, "it's so important, please."

"Tell him yourself, but don't be afraid of him. He'll turn you down if he sees signs of weakness. You won't lose anything by asking him." Her voice was gentle.

"I can't. Can't look him in the eye. I'll get confused when he starts asking questions."

"If it were up to me . . . It's his work and yours, not mine. When he starts it there's no reasoning with him until he finishes. I don't want to make him angry. He'll tell me not to interfere. He'll want to know why you didn't ask him yourself." She gathered the boy into her arms and stroked the back of his head and he did not resist her.

He shared a bed with Lázaro. When he got into it after bathing, Lázaro was still awake. "You tired, Laz?"

"Yeah, and we do the same tomorrow," he whispered.

64

"Shit! Think he'll let me go to the movies?"

"No! You know how he is. Don't even ask him."

"What's so important about doin' it tomorrow? It can wait! Why's he gotta be the first one through?"

"That's how he is!" Lázaro's tone scolded him. "He jus' has to be the first one through." He pulled at the blanket and widened the distance between him and Jaime.

"Damnit! Why does he have to be?" he spoke to him as if Lázaro were his father's apologist.

"You know! You like it too when all them people start sayin' how he does everything better'n anybody else!"

For a while neither said anything. Then Jaime spoke, his voice softer now, his anger controlled. "I wanna know who the Lone Ranger is. Tomorrow's the las' chapter. They only show it on Sunday. I seen the other fourteen."

"Fairy tales! That stuff's all made up!"

"What's the use of seein' the first fourteen chapters if I can't see the las' one? I been wastin' my time."

José María got up before dawn. His wife was already preparing breakfast and the food he and his sons would need for the day. He entered the kitchen and she turned to search his face; he did not look at her. He sat at the table and she served him a cup of coffee, adding milk and a teaspoon of sugar to it. He stirred it slowly before drinking.

"Did you get enough sleep?" she asked. "You didn't even move when I got in bed last night."

"*Sí*, more than enough." His face was impassive and the traces of sleep were all but gone from it.

Two fried eggs with lacy edges covered one half of the plate she set before him; the other held a steaming heap of *frijoles refritos*. "Is there much left to do?" she asked as she reached for the tortillas and *salsa picante* and put them on the table. Furtively, she studied his face.

"We've scarcely begun. We'll spend the day there."

"Don't you get tired?" she asked without hope.

"It doesn't matter. If we don't do the work, who will?"

He savored every mouthful, lowered his head to the plate to eat the running yolks. He cleaned his plate with a tortilla. When he finished he went to call them. It was dawning.

"Get up, *pronto!*" They sat up rubbing their eyes. "I'll go on ahead, don't be long." The door closed and he was gone.

When they got there he was working faster than the day before. The sun had not yet risen and they felt cold in their jackets. His black bike, like a horse, stood to one side of the shack. He waved and then gestured. From a hiding place in a wall of the shack Lázaro withdrew a big wrench wrapped in an oil-stained cloth—the fireplug wrench. Taking it and the gallon jugs, he and Jaime went to the fireplug just off Torrence Avenue. Their workday had started and they knew they would soon be warm. They would spend the day hoeing.

At noon they sat on the ground to eat. Jaime nibbled his taco, daydreaming. Lázaro ate with gusto. José María noticed Jaime's detachment and asked him with irritation, "Aren't you hungry?" His eyes riveted on the boy's.

"*Sí,*" he answered, shaken from his reverie. He tried to meet his father's gaze but couldn't.

"Then why don't you eat? Don't you feel well?"

"I'm all right, *papá,*" he answered, his eyes averted.

"Look at me when I talk to you! *¿Qué te pasa?*"

"I wanted . . . "

"What did you want?"

"I . . ."

"Out with it! I want to eat in peace."

"I wanted to go to the movies. They only show it today, I want to see it." His voice was unsteady.

"Movies? We have work to do! We'll have something to show for it later, something to eat!" The sharp tone of annoyance underpinned his words. "What did you want to see?"

"The Lone Ranger," he said meekly, thinking his father

was getting meaner and more impatient with the years.

"The Lone Ranger, *mierda*! Look at me! I'm the real Lone Ranger! And you're the real *Tonto*! Now eat!"

They were finishing their meal when José María pointed, saying, "Look, there's your Lone Ranger!" Jaime winced.

The man stood out clearly on a rise beyond hearing range. He wore black clothes, a big black hat, and carried stakes, twine and a hammer. Quickly, he marked off the boundaries of a good-sized plot of land.

"He's crazy," José María said when the man left. "It's too hard, the grass is too thick, he'll never finish."

A nap refreshed them and Jaime looked more relaxed. At day's end the three were happy to be going home—José María because he would finish turning over the ground the following day, the boys because they had to go to school and would have five days to rest. He sent them on ahead and locked up. On his bicycle he would catch and pass them along the way.

He returned from the *milpa* Monday evening to say he had finished hoeing. On Tuesday he burned grass and weeds and leveled and smoothed the earth for planting. In the evening he told them the Lone Ranger had given up spading— "*Ya se rajó.*" Lázaro smiled. On Wednesday, Thursday and Friday, while Lázaro and Jaime were in school, José María, a steel worker, labored in the mill. At dawn on Saturday they left together. Jaime and Lázaro carried small sacks of corn and onion bulbs, and a Warren hoe. José María had packets of seed, balls of twine, a hammer and food in a box tied to the carrier of the bike. "Hurry," he ordered them, "I'll be waiting for you," and rode off on his bicycle.

"Guess he'll get there pretty quick," Jaime said. "Yeah," Lázaro agreed, "there's no traffic. Come on, we better hurry." They began to run. When they got tired they walked, but only until they could catch their breath, then they ran again.

As José María approached the turnoff on Torrence Avenue, he suddenly stiffened, stopped pedaling and looked beyond the dirt road to the right. Inside the twine boundaries the land had been cleared and readied for planting. The man was working there. José María hurried to his shack, unlocked it, carried in the box and took what he needed to do his work—hammer, twine, stakes, a stick to measure with. He worked fast, drove in the stakes and ran the twine out close to the ground making parallel lines grow.

They came out of the tunnel, crossed 95th Street and ran on. From a distance they saw him moving like a shadow on the rise just beyond their *milpa* and were surprised.

"What's he doing up there?" asked Jaime, pointing.

"I don't know," the other answered.

They drew closer. The field was newly spaded. "Boy! He must have worked his ass off! Think Pa helped him? Maybe that's what he's doing up there," said Lázaro, confused.

"Look!" Jaime pointed. His father had just come out of the shack. The other figure stood up straight and the boys saw the big black hat.

When they reached him, José María cocked his head toward the field above and said, "That Lone Ranger sure knows how to work. ¡*Pronto*!" he urged. "Let's teach him a lesson!"

They made short work of the remaining stakes and twine, and while the boys went for seed, José María took the triangular hoe and began to cut shallow furrows in the earth under the taut lines. He paused to show them how to plant the seed, using the line to sight. They had heard it all before, seen him do it many times. Lázaro started at one end, Jaime at the other, and they met in the middle. The line came down but the stakes remained, would until sprouts appeared. Seed, line down, seed, line down. Again and again. He was pressing them now, closing the furrows with his Warren hoe, burying the seed with the right amount of soil, stopping only to instruct them when they finished with one kind of seed and were ready to start with another. They planted corn, onions, carrots, radishes. After lunch they would do the beets, coriander, string beans, peas, squash and cucumbers. The potatoes would come later, the peppers and tomatoes when it was warmer.

They ate quietly at noon. He was pleased with what they had done—more than if the Lone Ranger had not goaded him. When they finished their meal he told them, "We won't nap today." His eyes caught Jaime's surprised look. "Blame the Mexican Lone Ranger," he said, standing up. "We'll show him," he threatened, and the three went back to work.

Resentment choked Jaime. Why can't he stop ridin' me, he thought, it's bad enough I didn' see the las' chapter. He can teach Black Hat a lesson by hisself, I got nothin' against him. He should take it easy on us, we're jus' kids. Me an' Laz together, we could match him, maybe beat him. Let him try an' teach us a lesson. We'd show him.

The Lone Ranger left before they did. When they finished they went to see what he had done. He did not work as carefully as they. Up close his *milpa* was not as black as it looked from a distance. Clumps of grass dotted the field; they would be long in drying, might take hold and grow again. His rows were wavy, the earth not leveled. Still, he did better work than the *milperos* who already had plots and would come later. And they knew from experience that straight rows and neatness had nothing to do with yield.

It was still light but they were going home because they had run out of seed. "Take the wagon," he ordered, "we'll need it for the potatoes and bedding plants." They helped him get it out of the shack, then took over, pulling it as he walked away from them with his bike.

"Get on," Jamie told Lázaro when they reached the pavement, "I'll pull you a while." Torrence Avenue was smooth.

"Okay, I'll pull you later." He climbed on.

The wagon was lighter with the sides down. They didn't need them to move the bedding plants and potatoes. It would be easy to pull. Jaime leaned forward to get the wagon going, slowly moved his legs until he was walking, walked faster, stumbled, lost his momentum and had to start again. He got it up to a jog, no more, though he strained. He felt anger when he thought of how his father could fly with it, and then he tired and had to walk. They took turns all the way home.

Saturday night the temperature fell. On Sunday it was so cool that José María decided not to plant the tomatoes and peppers. A frost would kill them and he didn't want to risk it. But they would plant the potatoes. On the rough wooden floor of the shack, under his sons' gaze, he cut the tubers into pieces with eyes and then the three planted them. They would have potatoes for the whole year.

Black Hat did things his own way, well. But different from José María's. Core and detail were worked out all at once by José María. Black Hat went to the crux and handled the detail later. Jaime and Lázaro argued about this.

"It's better that way," Jaime said to Lázaro in defense of Black Hat's way of doing things. "We work and work 'til there's no more work, then we rest. He works and rests. I coulda seen the las' chapter of the Lone Ranger."

Lázaro disagreed. "Remember the year it did'n rain much an' we watered all the time? He would'n have time to go back if he had to water! An' remember the year it rained so much we could'n keep up with the weeds?" He hated the intruder.

Between the two men there was no exchange. Both held aloof, as if each thought the other should speak or wave first.

And each went about his work pretending to ignore the other, but each knew the other was there and took him into account. José María knew more, had more experience. Realizing this, the other man followed his lead.

"Did you see how he put in his tomatoes the day after Pa did?" Lázaro asked with disgust.

"Yeah, he's pretty smart," Jaime observed.

"Smart, shit! Copycat! Can't even do things hisself!"

"You jus' don't like him. What'd he ever do to you?"

"Why's he *here*? Comin' an' learnin' our secrets! Knows his stuff'll be safe 'cause we're here. Let him go over there where there's nothin'!" Lázaro fired his arm southwest.

"You're crazy! He can go anywhere he wants, jus' like us. He's a good worker, looks like Pa when he's workin', walks like him too, does'n he?"

"Bullshit! You're blind, you can't see!"

In May the Lone Ranger built a shack. A few *milperos* had shacks—scarecely more than was needed to store tools. In a sudden rain they could step inside to keep dry. José María's was more. He had built it with care, one large room just inside the door and two small ones off to the left. It had a wooden floor, asphalt roof and siding that he had salvaged from a wrecking site, and on the east side an overhanging roof that provided shade during most of the day. He was the only *milpero* who moved his family out there when school let out. His two oldest sons had neighborhood jobs and took care of the flat where they lived. For the Rivera's it was a *casita* rather than a shack. What the Lone Ranger built on an elevation in plain sight of José María's *casita* was his own *casita*. It was as big as the Rivera's, but newer and sturdier and had black asphalt roofing and siding.

"I told you he's a good worker, jus' look at that!"

"An' I told you he's a copycat! Built it right here as close to us as he could get! What's he scared of?"

"I woulda built it there too; it's the best spot!"

"Looks jus' like him, like his stupid hat! Dresses like somebody died. Why does'n he go away?"

"Yeah, it looks like him all right."

José María wondered if he would bring his family to live there. Lázaro frowned. Jaime smiled seeing how much he was like his father and how different, hoped he had a son his age.

The work was easier now, but they went every day for a while and it was hot. Wherever they found weeds encroaching they cut them down with their hoes. Around the base of the fast-growing plants they hilled the earth and the *milpa* took on a deep-furrowed look. When it was necessary, they watered, taking great care with the corn and tomatoes. There was always something to do. He went whenever he could—to inspect, give orders, and work when he had time. The boys put up a swing in front of the *casita* and he said nothing when he saw it. When he could, Jaime liked to swing there slowly, thinking of his friends at the YMCA, following the flight of birds and envying their freedom.

Early in June they were alone, weeding one end of a field of tomatoes. Jaime knew that when school let out his life would change—he would stop seeing his friends. Now more than ever he wanted to be with them, to join them in activities at the YMCA. He felt oppressed swinging the hoe, knowing he would spend every day of the summer on the *milpa*. It had been different before, when Lázaro had been companion enough for him and the vastness of nature had awed and absorbed him. A meadowlark sang—"throw your hoe away"— and he turned in sudden anger to look at Lázaro, who went on working.

Jaime reached into a plant and twisted off a tomato; it was green, hard. He gripped it, reared back and fired it at

Lázaro. Struck, Lázaro turned, saw the green ball at his feet, picked it up and met Jaime's belligerence with fury. "Prick!" he shouted and threw it hard. Jaime dodge it, grabbed at the ready supply of ammunition that surrounded him and began hurling. For several minutes they became mortal enemies firing green tomatoes at each other. Above them, flying in circles, a killdeer cried its alarm, "Kill dee, kill dee!"

It ended as suddenly as it had started and when they saw what they had done, fear sobered them. They scrambled to gather the green balls scattered over a wide area.

"Why'd you have to start it?" Lázaro scolded and lamented at the same time, his voice heavy with remorse.

"Why'd you throw it back?" Jaime snapped. "You're older an' should know better!"

"He'll be here in an hour! We still got weedin' to do an' all them tomatoes to pick up an' get rid of. He'll be madder'n hell if he finds out!"

They gathered the tomatoes in a sack, carried them off and buried them. When he arrived they were still weeding.

"Why haven't you finished?" he asked in anger. A look of alarm passed between them. He saw it and frowned.

"We got here late," Lázaro answered.

"¡*Huevones*!" His lips went hard and thin. "Idlers!"

The tomato plants were rooted in waves of soil that supported them. He walked through the rows inspecting as he went along, he backed up, bent over, touched, advanced slowly and finally exploded, "What happened here?"

"Nothing," Lázaro said.

"¡*Con una chingada*! What do you men nothing?" He turned to Jaime, "You, come here!" The boy ran. "¿*Qué pasó aquí*?"

"Nothing, *papá*," he answered with fear.

The man's hand shot out, caught the boy's hair, tightened and drew the head back slowly. "¿*Qué pasó aquí*?" he roared.

"We had a fight," Jaime confessed quickly. Instantaneously the man shoved the boy, knocking him over.

"Come and see!" he shouted to Lázaro. The boy paled as he ran to his father's side. "Look, goddamnit!" The man pointed to broken branches. "¡*Mira*!" He held up some yellow blossoms. "¡*Mira, con una chingada, mira*!" With his index finger he turned up stems that had held green fruit; the ends were still moist. "¡*Mira*!" He picked up a tomato they had missed. Enraged, he whirled and fired it at Jaime, who threw up his arms protectively. It struck him on the shoulder and split. Then he turned to Lázaro and kicked him with a lightning blow that caught his thigh and dropped him.

"Follow me!" he shouted. He stopped under a tree at the edge of the field. They watched him unbuckle his belt and snap it from his belt loops with a jerk, saw his jaw tighten when they stood beside him. "Who started it?" he asked.

"I did," came Jaime's answer.

He pulled the boy to him and asked, "How old are you?"

"I'm ten," he said, his eyes on the belt.

"¡*Agáchate*!" he ordered. Jaime bent over. The man raised his right arm and the boy's head spun around, his eyes straining over his left shoulder. "Don't look back!" The boy obeyed, the arm fell with vengeance and the belt exploded. Jaime straightened up, pulling in his rear as if someone had touched it with a branding iron.

"Count!" the man shouted.

"One!" came the anguished cry.

"¡*Agáchate*!" The belt came down harder. "Count!"

"Two!" Jaime straightened up and shifted his feet.

"Don't move!" The boy turned to look at him. "¡*Agáchate*! Is this what we busted our balls for?"

Lázaro watched without moving, his flesh cringing with each blow, his fear trapped on a track between his anus and his testicles, running back and forth, back and forth. He would get twelve. All this for a few minutes of madness.

"Get to work!" he ordered when it was over. "You stay here tonight and start working early in the morning! ¡*Huevones*!"

They were working when he mounted his bike and rode off, but they went on working, expecting him to come back, knowing he might sneak up on them. The sun set and he was nowhere in sight. At twilight the last *milperos* left and the boys went to their *casita*. Neither spoke. Both were hungry. They had no light; in a few minutes it would be black. Lázaro opened the door. The big wagon was on its side in the shack.

Jaime burst into tears and began kicking it desperately. "Fuckin' wagon, fuckin' no good shitty wagon!" He kicked it until he spent himself and the wagon withstood everything, scarcely moved under the torrent of blows.

"Let's get it outta the way," Lázaro urged, "jus' help me get the wheels down." Jaime refused.

Struggling, Lázaro stood it up and rolled it out of the way. "I'm gonna sleep on the wagon," he said. "Better find yourself a spot now, you won't be able to see." He handed Jaime an armful of sacks. "Ready?" he asked a moment later.

"No. It's okay, I'll lock the door," Jaime answered.

His bed made, Jaime went to the door, turned for a last look around the room, saw Lázaro stretched out on the wagon, closed the door and everything went black. He locked it and made his way back to his spot, lay down on his back and covered himself with the sacks. The image of Lázaro on the wagon burned in the darkness—he saw it on the ceiling and walls, wherever his eyes went. Gradually it dimmed and faded. "Laz . . . Laz . . . " he whispered. His brother was asleep. He imagined Lázaro dead and laid him out in a wooden box and the wagon came to mind and he laid him out on the wagon and buried them in a deep hole near the well. The vision frightened him. He struggled to drive it away and thought I'm the one who should die. It would be better, I wouldn't have to put up with all this. That damn wagon! If I could jus' die now an' wake up tomorrow all grown up, a man, if I . . .

Jaime opened his eyes. Blades of light were slitting the darkness. He slipped his hand into his pants, under his shorts, and touched his ass. It felt feverish to his fingertips, the tips cold to his ass. He had been so stupid the day before. Idiot! He had caused it all, it was his fault. And Lázaro had paid for it too. He could just make him out in the darkness and called to him, "Lázaro, Laz, get up, get up."

"What time is it?" a corrugated voice from the wagon asked.

"I don't know. Let's get up before he gets here."

"Okay." He heard Jaime get up, make his way across the floor and unlatch the wooden pane. When they moved into the shack his father would put in the glass windows and they would know what time it was. A hinge creaked and light rushed in. There was no sun in the pale blue sky.

Jaime put his head through the window. "Damn Black Hat!"

"He there already?" Lázaro asked.

"No. It's his shack. Looks jus' like the asshole, standin' up there like he owned everything."

"I thought you liked him, always stickin' up for him. You still think he looks like Pa?" Lázaro got down from the wagon and went to the window. From its height the black shack dominated everything. Yes, it looked like him.

"I did'n say I liked him, I said he's a good worker."

"¡*Chingao*!" Lázaro complained, rubbing his stomach. "I'm hungry an' there's nothing to eat!" He stretched, yawned and stamped his feet. Neither had undressed nor taken off his shoes. And neither thought of washing. They took their hoes.

"Wanna eat green tomatoes?" Jaime asked, his voice thin and playful, his face forcing a smile. He looked at the wagon and it seemed to have grown smaller.

They worked with speed and care so that everything would be right when he arrived.

"What d'you think he'll say when he comes?" Jaime asked.

"Ask what we done. Then he'll check it all."

"Think he'll say anything about yesterday?"

"Only if somethin' reminds him. You know how he is. He'll be mad and lookin' for somethin' to pick on."

"Yeah, I know. An' he'll be lookin' mean an' yellin'."

At sunrise they spotted him at the end of Torrence Avenue. Riding slower than usual and wearing black, he sat straight in the saddle and held his head high. They bent over and worked faster, glanced at him furtively lest he catch them observing him. He went right on where he should have turned off, and they looked at each other quizzically. He stopped at the edge of Black Hat's *milpa*, propped the bike against a bush and stepped into the *milpa*. Only then did they realize it was Black Hat. He was not wearing his hat.

"The copycat bought hisself a bike!" Lázaro complained.

"Long as he don't bother nobody he can do what he wants," Jaime said, seeming to defend him.

They watched him so intently that he noticed and turned to wave. Jaime waved back. Lázaro muttered, "¡*Chíngate*!"

He came later, a box tied to his carrier. They went on working. He gave them a long piercing whistle, then gestured. At the shack-end of the field he waited for them.

"Here, something to eat!" he said, handing them the box. "Did anything happen?"

"No, *papá*," Lázaro answered.

"Did you fuck anything up?"

"No, *papá*," he answered again.

"And you, Lone Ranger!" Jaime lowered his eyes. "Look at me! Do you still feel like fighting?"

77

"No, *papá*," Jaime answered in a steady voice.

"Eat!" He took Lázaro's hoe and walked off.

They opened the box under the overhanging roof and ate. Jaime looked across the field and saw the two men. His father stooped over and Black Hat did too. Then he straightened up and at once Black Hat did the same, as if the other man controlled him. Jaime had the sensation of seeing a distant hammer strike silently and hearing the bang immediately after.

A week before school let out, on a Friday, Jaime and Lázaro were watering. It had not rained for two weeks and they had to water each plant. There was no time for anything else. In the wagon were two fifty-gallon casks they filled at the fireplug and pulled to the edge of the field, where they poured the water into five-gallon cans and walked up and down the rows watering. On Saturday they began at dawn and worked until noon, pausing to eat after filling the casks. Their lunch finished, they went back to watering. When the barrels ran out they returned to the fireplug and discovered they did not have the wrench. They searched for it frantically, in vain. They must have left it beside the plug at noon. It was gone and they would have to tell him. They went to the well, filled the casks, continued to water and thought obsessively of the wrench—how would he take its loss?

He came at three-thirty, a half hour after the seven-to-three shift at the mill let out. He moved stiffly and his face had its severest look—obsidian in his eyes, jade at his jaw, his cheekbones higher than usual and his nostrils flared. He seemed taller, gaunt, said nothing and passed on quickly to see what they had done. He could find no fault with their work and it made him clench his jaws.

In the *casita* he changed into his work clothes. They waited outside. He came out buckling his belt. "Let's finish," he said to them, heading for the wagon. They followed. As the three began watering, a meadowlark poured out its song— three falling liquid notes, up on the fourth, and down again in a dulcet slur. It sang repeatedly, as if it would never stop. Jaime tried to dispel his fear. Then the water gave out and he ordered them to bring more. They did not move.

Lázaro stammered, "The wrench . . . *papá* . . . the wrench . . . we lost it . . . we couldn't find it."

"What?" his eyes flashed the rage he had struggled to control. For a moment he could not speak.

"We lost the wrench," the boy repeated.

"Come with me!" he bellowed.

The man grew with each stride, swelling with fury, the stiffness gone. They ran to keep up with him and followed him into the shack. He reached for a coil of rope, held one end fast and flung the rest to the floor. They watched him gather it up in long loops, tightening his hold when he finished.

He struck without warning, the loops crashing down on Lázaro like a splayed bolt of lightning, felling the shrieking boy. With great speed he struck him two more times and the boy curled into a ball, his head buried in his arms and hands. He jerked him to his feet and the boy turned his back to him. The loops battered him and the boy stumbled.

"What did you lose?" the man asked.

"The wrench," Lázaro gasped.

The word set the man off and he rained blows on the boy, driving him screaming against the walls. Jaime receded into a corner, the din filling his ears, his eyes round with terror. Involuntarily, Lázaro raised his hands to stay the rope.

"Take your hands away!"

The boy tried to but couldn't. Repeatedly the loops lashed his hands and arms until he pulled them away.

"How did you lose it?"

"I don't know . . . we forgot it," he stammered, gagging on tears and mucus.

Now the rope found the groaning boy's thighs and fell in a furious torrent, the free-swinging ends of the coils snapping viciously against the clothed flesh. The boy offered no resistance, sank to the floor and the man stopped. He picked him up and shoved him through the door. Jaime saw blood on his brother's trousers. Then the man turned to him.

"Come here!" The boy moved out of the corner. "Who lost the wrench?" the man roared.

"I don't know," he answered, standing very still.

The blow fell with lightning speed, but Jaime was ready and withstood it silently. The man hesitated for an instant and Jaime saw his contorted face. With redoubled fury the man rained coils on the boy until he knocked him down. He saw the boy struggling to hold back tears and cries and it enraged him.

"Cry, damn you! Cry or I'll kill you!"

The boy jumped to his feet gulping down mucus, tears, pain and cries so desperately that he seemed to be choking.

"Why can't you do things carefully?" The boy said nothing, bracing himself for the next onslaught. "Answer me, damnit!"

It came hard now, the last furious downpour, the rope whistling in the narrow room, loops and coils everywhere, battering the boy, who moaned, wailed, cried out. The man threw the rope down and seemed to rest.

"¡*A la chingada*!" he ordered. Jaime darted out.

They drew from the well until the water was gone, then turned to other tasks. At nightfall they started for home and he made them run all the way to keep up with him.

She heard the pounding and opened the door, saw in their faces that something terrible had happened. Words would make things worse. She turned to him in silence for an explanation and he spat a command at her: "Feed them and send them to bed!"

"They need a bath," she objected.

"No! Feed them and send them to bed! *¡Pronto!*"

"What's wrong?" she asked solicitously.

"Ask them!"

They heard his alarm clock and got up stiffly. In the kitchen their mother was roasting peppers on the flame of the gas stove and the pungent aroma reached them. Jaime closed the bedroom door and turned on the light. They were stunned by what they saw—outrageously swollen thighs, darkly gnarled with welts and bruises. On Lázaro's right thigh there were crusts of blood where the flesh had been torn. They said nothing, looked at each other and themselves.

Jaime smiled awkwardly, whispered, "You look like a Mountie, Laz. You got the pants, meat pants, jus' need the boots."

"Yeah, you too." His voice was uneven. "Guess you can't be the Lone Ranger now," he added for a long silence.

Their fingertips gingerly testing wounded flesh, they were examining their thighs when the door opened. He stopped short, surprised to see them up. "*¡Pronto!*" he said, his eyes dropping fleetingly to their thighs, "I want you to eat and leave!"

In the kitchen nobody spoke. They ate quickly. At the door she handed them a lunch, embraced and kissed them, tried to smile, and in a steady voice said, "Off with you now, and behave." They nodded. He was eating.

They stepped into the cool morning, free of him until three-thirty. It was Sunday, too early for anyone to be up.

"Do your legs hurt when you walk?" Jaime asked.

"A little. It ain't bad. I thought it'd be worse."

They walked on, the only sound their voices, and their feet striking the pavement. Near the tavern at 88th Street Jaime found a book of matches and put it in his pocket.

"He ain't got no right doin' that to us," Jaime said.

Lázaro faced him in disbelief, "He's our father!"

"No right at all! He coulda killed us!"

A dog dragging its leash cut across their path, paused to look at them and moved on, following its nose.

"WE lost the wrench," Lázaro explained.

"That time he lost the money, nobody hit him."

"His money! Besides, it ain't the same."

"It's the same! It's always the same! He's right an' we're wrong an' he beats us to prove it!"

"You don't even know what you're sayin'! When you're married an' got kids you'll beat 'em too to teach 'em right."

"I ain't gettin' married an' I ain't havin' no kids!"

"We got off easy with the tomatoes an' you know it."

"That was over an' done! We paid for that one!"

"But you know it wasn't enough. Maybe he remembered it. Maybe somebody said somethin' to him at work. You know how he gets when they ask him if we're gonna work in the mill."

"Well I ain't forgettin' it!" Jaime's voice quavered. He wept. "I'll tell him, I'll never let him forget, never!"

They came out of the tunnel and crossed 95th Street. There were no cars. The *milpas* spread out before them—to the west they reached a distant line of trees; to the south they were bounded by Black Hat's plot. From the top of the elevation on which it stood the black shack dominated the whole extension. It was blacker, more imposing in the thin light.

"Goddamn Black Hat, jus' standin' there," Jaime said.

Lázaro nodded, knew his brother meant the shack. "Think he's got kids?" he asked Jaime.

"Yeah, bet he beats 'em too."

Jaime watched Black Hat grow, get bigger as they got closer. He kept staring at it and when they reached their shack he felt drawn to investigate, so much had it grown.

"Laz, let's go see Black Hat, there' no one around."

"What's there to see? Jus' a shack. Prob'ly locked."

"Let's go anyway. Before we start, okay?"

They could see better from the elevation—*milpas*, buildings in the distance, everything. Along Torrence Avenue there were no cars. They circled the shack.

"Look, the asshole's got no windows," Lázaro criticized.

"Asshole is right. I thought they were on this side."

They approached the door. A padlock hung from the hasp. Moving away from the shack, Lázaro chided Jaime, "We got work to do, let's go. There's nothin' to see here."

"Okay," Jaime answered, reaching for the lock. He jerked it and it gave. "Hey Laz, look, it's open!" He held it up.

Cautiously, they opened the door and stepped into a single room with a wooden floor. Against one wall there was a mattress, a jug of water beside it. In the corner near the door were his tools. Across the room, a table with a small kerosene stove at one end of it, candles, pans and some dishes at its other end. Against the other wall, two chairs. Behind the door they found a can of kerosene and a twenty-pound drum of lard. In the far corner a lidded metal box held dry food. The room was clean, neat, dark.

"Not much, is there?" Lázaro said.

"No. What Pa would have if he was out here alone."

"Bullshit! What about the wagon?"

"Yeah! Damn wagon! Got us into all that trouble yesterday. Damn place! Always bustin' our balls here! The asshole's prob'ly got a wagon too. At home!"

Lázaro grew uneasy and started through the door. Outside he stopped to say, "Let's go, someone will see us here."

"I'm comin'," Jaime said. He paused to close the door, replaced the lock, passed several feet beyond, whirled to look at the shack, spat at it and, sticking his hands in his pockets, yelled, "*Chíngate*, Lone Ranger!" Suddenly he stopped.

Lázaro saw him go back, enter for a minute and then come racing out as fast as he could go. "Run! Run!" Jaime warned. They did not stop until they were under the overhanging roof, and when they looked back a wisp of smoke was rising from the shack. Still breathing hard, they watched with big eyes as the smoke grew thicker. In the sky above the shack a bird wheeled and zigzagged on strong wings, its spasmodic flight now describing tight circles, now wide ones, its alarmed "Kill dee, killl deee," soft or loud as the bird rose or fell in the sky.

"Why'd you have to do that?" Lázaro reproved. Jaime was silent. "What'd the poor guy do to you? I did'n like him neither, but I never coulda done that. It ain't right!"

"I jus' did it, I don't know why!"

Against the pale blue of the early morning the shack burst into blood-red flame and groaned as it gave up a ferocious ball of black smoke. Jaime recoiled. Dimly he sensed that something momentous had happened, and he tried to smile through his uncertainty. Then he forced a laugh, and finally he shouted, waving his fist, "Copycat! Goddamn copycat! You shoulda been yourself 'steada someone else! Lousy copycat! We did'n want you aroun' here!"

The bird rose higher, its wings beating furiously, its alarm shrill and triumphant, "Killl deee, killl deee, killl deee!" Jaime followed it with his eyes as he settled into the swing and began to rock gently back and forth.

Octavo

Friday morning. You have been at your lessons for almost an hour. You and the other boys grow more and more restless—eyes shift, lips move, smiles flash, bodies stiffen. Something is up and you don't know what, not yet, but that doesn't keep you from taking part. Whatever it is, the girls are excluded, that much you know.

I can see everything from here, everything except their stomachs—those desks get in the way. If they knew how much I can see they'd be more careful. Something's going on. Just pretend I don't know, that I'm working on these papers. I'll catch them. There! There it is again. There's another. Signals. What do they mean? Only the boys, not the girls.

Something is pricking you beyond endurance, rising inside of you and looking for a way out. You watch Jorge. He glances at Mrs. Morgan, times his move perfectly and flashes the cover of his little book. A shiver stirs those of you who see it and you squirm with impatience, fidget in your seats. He does it again. Frank sees it and he does the same, flashes his. The excitement mounts. They're new eight-pagers and all of you want to see them. What the two do becomes more dangerous and exhilarating with each repetition, for all of you.

What is it? Just look at them, all of them, they'll wet their pants if they keep this up. They're watching me now, carefully. Whatever it is, I'm just missing it. But I have to pretend or I'll scare them off. Maybe they drank too much water this morning. That game—"Let's see who can drink the most water." God. I was never that way, I don't think I was. Who is the ringleader here? Probably Frank. One slip, just one.

Your excitement is like the one you feel when the teacher leaves the room for a few minutes and you, the boys, compete in rushing recitations of old rhymes made new, the object of your contest being to finish what you're reciting before the teacher returns, and to shock the girls:

" . . . Jack jump over the tip of my dick."

" . . . You ain't sick an' you ain't dead, all you need is pussy in bed."

" . . . He put in his rod an' shot off his wad an' said what a good boy am I."

" . . . With two big balls anna cock that crawls an' pretty maids all in a row."

Thank God for the bell! Sometimes I think I'm going crazy. "Stop! Stop!" Just look at them. "Go back to your desks and wait until I give you permission to leave. You boys! What's the rush? You almost trampled the girls. All right, you can leave now. Take it easy, take it easy! No roughhousing or I'll take you to the principal's office!"

("Ole man Fitts hadda pimple on his dick . . . ")

You crash through the door of the restroom, all of you. A big, high-ceilinged room with large windows and wide urinals. Just inside the door there is a metal shield that blocks the view of passersby in the hall. Frank and Jorge plant themselves between the sinks and toilets, away from the entrance. The rest of you swarm around them and the mirror doubles your number. "Gitcher two cents ready," Frank orders. He sticks out his hand before letting go of the little book. "Yeah, an' stop shovin' back there, you'll gitcher turn," Jorge adds, holding on to his too. You lean forward, your necks stretched as far as they can, on tiptoes those of you at the edge of the swarm. Jorge, "Money talks first," and he shoves his hand at you. Frank, "Yeah, an' keep your voices down, someone's gonna hear us." One of you, "Shit! I only got two cents!"

Frank, "That's okay, but you'll have to see 'em last." The eight-pagers pass among you, from hand to hand, back and forth, round and round, each of you squeezing hard, flipping the pages forward and back, intent on getting your money's worth. Jorge, "Don't pull it so hard, you'll tear it!" One of you, "I'm next! Tell 'em, Jorge, here, here's my money." Your voices fill the room.

What the hell's going on there, I can hear them through the closed door. They should be on the playground. I'd better see what it is. "All right in there, out to the playground immediately or I'll come in and haul every one of you down to the principal's office."

(". . . So he caught the teacher nex' door . . . ")

You hear a sharp rap on the door, see it open a crack and then hear her voice. You bolt toward the door, tumble through it, speed to the stairwell and descend in leaps of three and four stairs. When you reach the bottom you look up and see Mrs. Dorn shaking her head and mumbling something. You rush out of the building, to the playground. Frank and Jorge make you scatter. It's too risky on the playground, too hard to control a crowd and the eight-pagers. One of the older boys— an eighth grader or second-semester seventh grader—might snatch them from you and there would be no way of getting them back. Outside you must do it quietly and only with a couple of guys. The bell rings. Recess is over and you head for the building.

They seem more settled now. I wonder what it was. All that pent up energy. Maybe I can relax now.

After lunch you are calmer. The morning's rolling boil is gone, the wild bursting of bubbles struggling to escape from your blood. You simmer in your juices now, the heat under control. You have returned with old eight-pagers rescued from hiding places. More restrained, you will pass them around, without pay, and by day's end, tomorrow at most, they will have burned off your urge. And your blood will move as before, the eight-pagers will return to their hiding places to stay there until you need them again. In class your behavior is mischievous, not feverish. One of you lobs a spitball. Three of you drop books to the floor in a deliberate rhythm. You see Mrs. Morgan frown. You make silence. Frank honks his nose into a blue cloth, once, twice. One of you laughs.

"I've had enough of you! Behave! All of you!" They're testing me. Not as bad as this morning but I can't let them get away with it. "The next one to step out of line goes directly to the principal's office. I don't care who you are."

(". . . He laid her on a bowl . . . ")

You put an end to your shenanigans. You know she's tough when she has to be. Fair always, and reasonable for a teacher, and you like her for this. She's not like Mrs. Dorn. But you know when to stop.

They've given me a headache. I don't want to lose my patience, my temper with them. Best to stop them now. "I've put up with your nonsense all day and I'm sick of it! I try to ignore you and you get worse. I mean you boys! I give you an inch and you take a mile. Well, I'm drawing the line. Step over it and the next stop is the principal's office."

(". . . An' shoved it up her hole . . . ")

The recess bell sounds and you race for the door. Mrs. Morgan warns you, "Take it easy! What's so urgent that you have to trample each other half to death?" You spill into the hall and charge to the restroom. You are so eager to get in that you don't see Mrs. Morgan standing at her door, waiting, looking your way.

God! It's good for them to get out and run awhile. For me too. It's that time of the year. They're no different from the trees, sap flowing and buds popping along their branches. Lots of noise in there. A little running on the playground is all they need.

In the restroom a number of you pull out your eight-pagers. The rest of you cluster around, others joining you as they enter. You whistle, hoot, exclaim. "Keep the noise down!" one of you commands. The noise ebbs. "Wow! Lookit Jiggs with all them bare-ass girls! He tole Maggie he was gonna play cards at Dinty's." . . . "An' look! He's still smokin' his cigar!" . . . "She'll fix his ass if she catches him!" . . . "Not when she's doin' that! Goddam Maggie! Right in the rockin' chair wi' the butler!" . . . "Boy! Jus' lookit them knockers! ¡*Chingao*!" . . . In another corner you follow the exploits of Popeye. "Looks jus' like his arm, don't it?" . . . "An look what happens to it when he eats a can of spinach! It's bigger'n his arm!" . . . "Lookit Olive Oil! Like two peas on a bread board." . . . "Yeah! An' a little steel wool down below!" . . ."Bet Mrs. Brandt looks jus' like that!" You all howl. In another group Dick Tracy holds your attention. "*That's* why his name's Dick! Looks like a small cannon to me." "All them lady crooks! An' he gits paid fer that? I'd be a cop too!" "Hey! That fat one looks like Mrs. Dorn, don't she?" Explosions of laughter . . . Tarzan and Jane. Mutt and Jeff. Alley Oop. Smokey Stover. Blondie . . .

What's taking them so long? And that damned noise. Something's going on there, I'd better check. Do it quietly, maybe I can hear . . . God! Ella, she'll know what to do.

Unbelieving, you see Mrs. Dorn and Mrs. Morgan invade your washroom without warning and catch you unawares. Paralyzed, you watch each of them snatch an eight-pager from you.

"What is this? I want . . . God! You filthy little animals! Peggy, did you . . . " "Yes, Ella. No wonder they didn't come out. They belong in the toilet!"

You watch Mrs. Dorn's eyes goggle. You say nothing. There is no need to say anything. You see Mrs. Morgan examine the other one, unblinkingly, a faint smile on her face. And then Mrs. Dorn catches you unawares again.

"I want every one of these *things*, every one! Quickly! Unless you want me to drag every last one of you down to the principal's office!"

(" . . . An' never hadda pimple any more.")

On the playground you sit against the cyclone fence and brood over your loss. A chanting voice reaches you, "Ole man Fitts hadda pimple on his dick/So he caught the teachers nex' door . . . " "Shit! It was brannew!" Frank protests. "Did'n anyone of you see 'em come in? Was'n anyone watchin'?" "We saw 'em when you did," one of you explains . . . "They're not suppose' to do that, go inna boy's toilet like that. It's trespassin' an' you c'n git in trouble for that. Maybe we otta tell ole man Fitts." "Don't be stupid! He'll expel us if they tell him what we were doin'." "They wannida see cocks! Did'n you see me takin' a piss when they come in, an' did'n you see how they looked at me? Boy, they mus' be really hard up!" "You're fulla shit! Who'd wanna see yer goddam raisin? If they wannida see cock they woulda came in when I was pissin'." The bell rings the end of recess. You, those who lost your eight-pagers, look at one another and don't move. You have five minutes to get to class, and you don't want to return. But you have to. You start back, dragging your feet, kicking gravel as you go, nervous about returning because you don't know what to expect. Jorge, "Think ole man Fitts'll be there?" Frank, "Who knows! We're screwed either way. If he's there he'll do somethin' to us. If he ain't, them two'll have it in fer us fer the rest of the year. They got us over a bowl, like Fitts's got them!" You enter the building full of misgivings, quietly climb the stairs. You want to disappear into the walls, be reduced to insects, anything that will get you past the trio of teachers standing just beyond the top of the stairs, in the middle of the hall. You feel yourself grow as you approach them.

Why do we have to stand here doing this? And why did they tell *me*? I didn't have anything to do with it! And I don't want to! "Look, look at this one!" Laughing here, right out in the open, they must be crazy. "What do you think of this one, Carolyn?" I hope I never get like them, never. "I wish they showed as much interest in their school work."

The bell rings and Mrs. Morgan does not enter. They are still in the hall and you can hear their muffled voices and laughter. You are stunned, confused. What you saw, it isn't true, couldn't be. Are they really standing in the middle of the hall doing exactly what you and the others were doing in the boy's room? They didn't even see you go past them, they were so absorbed in your eight-pagers! You try to understand, especially you, Jorge, and you turn, catch Frank's attention and thrust up your chin asking for an explanation. You, Frank, throw up your hands and shrug your shoulders. You think of the three, so different, and yet the same out there. You shake your head. Mrs. Morgan is all curves and sweet smells. She's fair with you, more than the others, and patient. Pretty face, nice lips, soft eyes, beautiful red hair. When she gets very close to you, you go to pieces, all of you. She likes to sing and laugh. Mrs. Dorn is a fatso. Those big tits go as far forward as that big ass goes backward. Rocks when she walks, like someone was using her for a tug-a-war. Gruff voice, grating and loud. Doesn't trust you, never does. Mrs. Brandt, the youngest of the three. Skinny, narrow hips, little thin lips. Her mouth looks like a slit under her nose. Right hand always at her mouth, covering it or reaching into it with thumb and index finger, searching for something that keeps falling in. Talks through her nose and complains about everything. And nervous, always fidgety. Mrs. Morgan enters.

It's like a cemetery in here! That really took care of them. They're ashamed to look up here. Or afraid. Wait'll I show them to Harold. God! He'll laugh, I know it, he'll die laughing. Shouldn't let them see me smiling.

At three o'clock the bell rings the end of the school day. You leave quietly. You, Frank, stay. You're not afraid or confused anymore. You approach Mrs. Morgan and ask her, "When do I get the books?" She looks at you for a moment. Her face gets hard.

The ringleader, I was right. Smart aleck, I'll show you. "If you ever mention this again I will personally take you home and tell your parents the whole story. Do you understand? Now get out of here!"

Outside they are waiting for you. You spit the words out, "Goddamn crook! She won't give 'em back, never! They cost money an' they ain't easy to get! . . . Goddamn pig! She prob'ly wantsa study 'em so she can do it inna rockin' chair with her ole man! Like Maggie an' the butler." You, Jorge, speak right up, "Naw! Don't say that about her! She ain't like that! She treats us right, not like the others, an' you know it. An' she doesn't need them eight-pagers for nothin'!"

"Frank's right! They otta pay us fer our books if they're gonna look at 'em an' laugh! No one's gonna tell me Fat an' Skinny ain't learnin' stuff from 'em! That's why they didn't take them to Fitts! They wannida learn!" All of you have something to say now, something to shout at one another, something condemning. You, Jorge, drown out the others, "That's hor'shit, you dummies! Anybody knows why they did'n take 'em to Fitts—he's a big pussy hound! They did'n wanna give him no ideas about screwin' new ways 'cause he'd git notions an' they gotta screw or lose their job. Whadda you think that pimple-on-his-dick stuff's all about?

You dummies! . . . " The clarity of Jorge's explanation chokes off your words, you understand now.

In silence you break up and drift in several directions. A few of you go home feeling good, thinking Dorn and Brandt deserve everything Fitts does to them. The rest of you go home feeling terrible, knowing that Fitts—that bastard Fitts!—gets to Mrs. Morgan.

"Learn! Learn!"

José María Rivera always read important letters with a red pencil in his hand. They were letters written in *castellano*—he sometimes called it *cristiano*, his eyes rolling, his voice serious—by people who knew or should have known the language as well or better than he did, which is what made the letters important. He read first for spelling errors, rapidly, crossing out, adding, changing, circling, then he went back for a second reading to seize anything that had escaped his initial sweep. In repeated readings, finally, he concentrated on what the letters said.

There were few of these letters in the passing of a year. The two or three his brothers-in-law far off in Mexico wrote to his wife, letters that always provoked him to say in a louder than normal voice, "*Lástima de educación universitaria, no saben escribir.*" A pity indeed, he never tired of thinking, they were educated at the university and just didn't know how to write. He said it as much to himself as to his wife, a perceptive woman who did not answer him. Years ago, before leaving Mexico, he had already developed the habit of saying things aloud to himself. And there were the other letters, rare strikes that came into his hands from friends who did not quite understand them, and from the friends of friends.

Chema—his friends called him that—had long ago stopped "editing" the *barrio semanarios*, weeklies. They had too many errors, the same ones over and over and they held no challenge for him. Besides, his anonymous letters to their editors had gone unheeded and he was not interested in writers who did not want to be redeemed. "*Cabrones ojetes*, damned assholes," he had labeled them in the final letter, and as he wrote he shouted repeatedly to himself, "*¡Que se*

94

chinguen ésos! Fuck them! *¡No tienen interés en aprender!* They're not interested in learning!"

The church bulletin of Our Lady of Guadalupe was another matter. The Riveras, whose destinies were in the hands of *don José*—his acquaintances called him that—were not church-going, but every Sunday *don* José sent one of his sons for the bulletin, warning him as he left, to be careful, "*Ten cuidado*," and not to get lost in that den of corruption, "*No te vayas a perder en ese recinto de perversos*." Although the bulletin dealt exclusively with what Chema called "*cosas de beatas y maricones*, news for overly pious women and fairies"—births, marriages, deaths, baptisms, confirmations, first communions, fund-raising events, the activities of the Daughters of Our Most Holy Virgin of Guadalupe and of the Knights of the Virgin of Guadalupe—he acknowledged the excellence of its language, an excellence that was not without faults, however. The author of that bulletin was the *párroco*, Father Tortas, a Spaniard whom Chema called, "that overstuffed *gachupín*," adding gleefully, "*Cuervo cargado de carnes y de cagada*, a crow bursting with flesh and shit."

José María mined every one of Father Tortas' bulletins, and every one yielded something, however small or imagined. But it was the nugget of indisputable error that filled him with intense pleasure and made him shout, "*Aprende de tu padre, sanguijuela*, learn from your master, parasite! This is your only creative act, it should be perfect! You have nothing else to do, *manos de señorita*! ¡Aprende! ¡Aprende! Learn! Learn! If I am the only one willing to kick your ass, so be it! Your voice is louder than it should be, you must answer for it!" And José María taught the priest as well as he could, in anonymous letters that went out often but not regularly, for not all bulletins merited a complete letter. His sons, feeling themselves partners in this enterprise, delivered them to the church or the rectory, clandestinely, provocatively, under cover of the large crowds that moved in and out of the former or passed slowly by the latter.

There was no question of it, Father Tortas heeded portions of the anonymous letters and this made José María a better critic. Their conflict, the tip of the iceberg of their antagonisms, took place at the level of orthography, grammar, syntax, semantics. Sometimes José María applauded the priest's responses to particular challenges, for he would counter his unknown antagonist's thrusts with an ingenious verbal maze here, an extraordinarily subtle play on words there. At times the priest seemed to tweak his unknown critic by slipping into flagrant error. Chema begrudged the priest his mastery of the language and whispered to himself, "*Sí, dominas el castellano, pinche cura maricón*, you lousy fairy of a priest, you do know the language! You have this over my brothers-in-law, that wherever the hell they taught you, they taught you well, *manos de señorita*."

Juan Ginés Tortas' parishioners had never seen hands more beautiful than his. They had made José María think of the hands of figures in religious calendars. They were white, very white, the fingers slender and long and tapering into flat tips capped by manicured nails, a labyrinth of pale blue lines just under the skin. Hands surprisingly fleshless, firm and smooth. To his flock they seemed hands made for holding and displaying Christ, a living monstrance. Nearing fifty, Father Tortas was a big man with a bald pate. A sprinkle of white flakes fell from the hair that ringed his head, and his hands recurrently fluttered up to his shoulders to flick at the incessant snow. He dressed with an elegance that belied the notion that a priest's wardrobe is uniformly dull, and even his cassocks and robes were tailored to his personal desires. He had long ago assumed the practice, after Mass, of keeping his robes on and wearing them in his chambers. They intimidated parishioners he received there, giving him the distance he needed.

As seminarian and newly ordained priest, Juan Ginés, proud and serious by nature and gregarious by design, had been a competitor whose incentive was competition. He was a performer who excelled when he was surrounded by excellent performers. Drawn to material comfort, he had aspired to a position of prestige in some chancery, convinced that there he would find abundance and intellectual stimulation. But the young priest's impatience, buttressed by ambition and a knowledge of English, had driven him to the United States. He had imagined himself the Sepúlveda of the *mestizos* in Anglo-America, had envisioned himself in the American Hierarchy as the exegete of the Spanish-American text.

In the United States Juan Ginés saw the Canaan of his expectations crumble in the Babylon of his captivity in South Chicago. They had not told him as he would later tell himself—"¡*Me enviaron al culo de esta ciudad salchichera*!"—that South Chicago was the anus of sausage-making Chicago. He had come to a dead end when the world had seemed new to him, and for a time he had struggled to check his bitterness, winning small victories over his pride and ambition, but he could not vanquish them. He convinced himself that he had been intentionally misled, ultimately believing that they had exiled him unjustly. So it was that he made a sword of his disillusionment and a shield of what had been his expectations. His weight increased with his cynicism and his hair began to thin.

For more than twenty years Father Tortas had grieved the impatience that had led him to abandon Spain for the hope of rapid advancement in a city where, he discovered, it was reserved for priests with Irish surnames. Since then he had moved cautiously, slowly weighing alternatives on the scales of his distrust to arrive at decisions of consequence and inconsequence alike. He had pondered as long over the advisability of forming a parish baseball team as he had over the need for a second assistant. He scorned young people for their immaturity and lack of judgment, making them the target of diatribes delivered from the pulpit, subjecting them to inquisitional indignities in the intimacy of the confessional. And for more than twenty years he had indulged his pride with fantasies of what he could have been had he stayed in Spain: now a cardinal's secretary, now a bishop, now a cardinal. He became aloof, solitary, performed his duties with the aid of many, but drew nobody close to him and drew close to nobody, not even his assistant priests. Alone, he lived more in the world of what could have been than in the community where he ran out his time. What little affection he could summon he bestowed on his altar boys, who, uneasy in his presence, would not have passed their thirteenth year if he could have controlled their growth. Of his pastoral concerns in recent years only the composition of the church bulletin seemed to interest him. Not even his housekeeper really knew him.

On Saturday mornings Father Tortas sat at his desk and unhurriedly wrote the weekly bulletin on oversized sheets of lined paper. Working from a pad of notes, dates, symbols, he finished it in an hour, needing more time only if the bulletin was unusually long. But it never took more than two hours. His penmanship was clear, large and angular, marked by that stiffness characteristic of certain European hands. Typed by a volunteer whom the *párroco* had trained, the copy was taken to a local printer by noon and the finished product was delivered to the rectory before five. Chema's anonymous letters effected no obvious change in his routine. The priest gradually intensified his concentration, paid greater attention to expression, turned increasingly to figurative language, adopted a more sophisticated syntax and, except for rare instances, did not need additional time to produce the bulletin. Had he known this, José María, like those who measure others against themselves, would have been astounded by the facility and speed with which Father Tortas composed the document.

Like most of the men in the neighborhood, Chema worked in the steel mill. He was skilled at executing a variety of difficult and dangerous jobs that required strength, stamina and alertness. He did the jobs superbly, with an animal intelligence and grace that were incomparable among his fellow workers. He followed his nature in what he did, and what he did and how he did it were his only security in the mill since it was not unionized. But the work did not spend him; it failed to test his physical limits. It did not drain him of that need he felt to exhaust his energies. It failed to challenge his intelligence and he knew it always would.

Even the letters he wrote in English deserved at least one draft, and Chema composed them as well as he could. Inevitably he turned to one of his sons for help, a recourse that pained them both since José María had to accept his son's judgment and the son had to suffer his father's detailed, time-consuming explanations.

"But you can't say that, that's Spanish, it's not said like that in English," his son explained to him in Spanish.

"Who says you can't? If you understand what you're doing you can do anything you want to with language. But you don't understand! *¡Lástima! ¡Aprende! ¡Aprende!*"

"I'm tellin' you, Pa, *no es inglés*."

In some cases the son's advice was rejected. Having labored for an expression he thought poetic—"My determination to become a citizen is not different from the determination of the lion that, crippled, accepted Daniel's aid. My allegiance to the Daniel that is the United States could not be different from that of the lion to Daniel"—José María held fast to his creation over his son's protests, convinced that an adult would see what the youth had failed to appreciate. There was no antagonism between father and son, no rivalry, no dispute as to who knew English better. Both felt impatience: the father over his son's incomprehension of figurative language, the son over his father's insistence, which pulled ambivalently at the boy, who admired it even while it annoyed him. Together they hammered out a finished product and Chema then typed it, his fingers slowly pounding the keys of a winged, flightless Oliver. Chema was confident that the typewritten letter would impress its *gringo* reader.

But when José María wrote the most important letters, when he wrote letters in *castellano*—his own, his wife's—he prepared for the undertaking as carefully as Father Tortas might have readied everything for a Solemn High Mass. He spread newspaper over one end of the kitchen table to smooth its uneven surface, placed Bello's *Gramática de la lengua castellana* at his left elbow, a dictionary at his right, a half dozen sharp-pointed pencils and a block of unlined paper in front of him. His hands had worn through the covers of both books and he had skillfully rebuilt them. The dictionary was small, a desk copy often inadequate to his needs.

Imagining himself the addressee, José María gave himself selfishly to his letter, writing in intense pursuit of the perfection his mind projected just beyond his pencils. Always, after several days, he came close enough to that perfection to feel satisfied; on rare occasions he achieved it. Almost as a rule of thumb, the number of drafts his letters required equaled the number of pages per letter. His prose was solid, heavy at times, but he wielded it with ease and could make it leap and turn to his wishes. An isolated sentence might seem cumbrous, but it lost this quality in the configuration of a paragraph or passage. He shaped his prose as a blacksmith from Guanajuato fashioned wrought iron, heating it in the forge of his brain, hammering it over and over on the anvil of his judgement, plunging it finally into the cold water of acceptance, piece by piece, the overall design held in the eye of his intelligence. He read all finished letters to his wife:

Priest,

I repeat what I have told you before: you have no imagination. Inasmuch as you refuse to think of your parishioners as human beings, as *hermanos* or *hijos*, insisting, rather, on seeing them as animals, *ovejas*, always *ovejas*, lend consistency, unity, to your vision by seeing yourself as a sheep dog rather than as a shepherd. At least give your parishioners a little variety. Call them fish, or doves, or better still, *burros*. You, of all people, must know how important, useful and docile *burros* are in the Hispanic world as well as in the bible. Read Vargas Vila, for you might learn from him how . . . .

On the second page of your bulletin, first paragraph of the section entitled BAPTISMS, you employ a passive construction incorrectly. I bring to your attention that in passive constructions with se it is the nature of the passive subject that determines the form the verb must take . . . .

The tools of Chema's mill work—hammers, pickaxes, pokers, shovels, drills, wrenches—had made his hands hard and his fingers were rooted in a ridge of calluses that spread to the base of his thick palms. His nails were dense, horny, a little longer than those of other men who did his kind of work. To shake his hand was to shake the hand of a man wearing a gauntlet. In that hand a pencil or pen seemed to grow small, almost disappearing in his fist, so that when he wrote, the script seemed to flow from a little tube he operated with the slight pressure of three fingers.

The writing was utterly controlled, swift, rhythmically

winding and unwinding in fluid curves, the tall letters, all the same height, gracefully swayed from lower left to upper right, the crosses of the t's straight and slightly lengthened. It was elegant in its proportions, in the purity of its lines, in the inventiveness of its capital letters, in the almost-flourishes of occasional final letters that caught the eye with their air of effortless improvisation. The surprise of those who saw him write filled Chema with immense satisfaction, and he seized every opportunity to write that presented itself, even if it was only to sign his name. His Spanish letters were written in longhand. Nothing else would do.

He wrote with a Schaeffer fountain pen, white-dotted, medium point, in his judgment the finest writing instrument his money could buy. Several times a week he filled pages of a notebook with circles, ovals, straight and curved lines, all joined together and exactly alike. It gave him no pleasure to do these exercises. He performed them routinely, knowing that by doing them his hand would always be fully in control. On the subject of writing he spoke like a specialist:

"You hold the pen with little pressure, *apenitas*, about an inch and a half up from the point. The upper part rests in the cradle formed by the thumb and the index finger, *así*. And remember, this is the most important part, you write with the forearm, not with the wrist, *con el antebrazo*. The movement is from the elbow down, that way you never get tired. ¡*Nunca*! And the test is in how loosely you hold the pen. Go ahead, pull it from between my fingers, you'll see how easy it is to do. You see! ¡*Aprende, aprende*!"

The Rivera children all wrote well. José María had seen to that. They regularly did exercises for him in notebooks, but none showed the signs of calligraphic precociousness he had shown when he was their age. And they spoke well enough, both languages, but especially Spanish. They spoke it better than their friends, which did not surprise José María, for he had convinced them that it was important to speak well. They had heard him dominate conversations with his friends, had heard the latter turn to their father to settle disputes about word meanings, had seen him reach for his dictionary to drive all doubt from the minds of his listeners.

As much as anything it was the dictionary test that impressed the Rivera children. José María did it not to show off but as a measure of himself in the presence of his children, as a way of showing them that they could learn as he had. He handed them his dictionary and they took turns opening it at random and reading him words that looked difficult. He would define them. He did it to show them that words belonged to anyone who wanted them, and they came to believe that success in life and the power of speech were closely linked, that one could not be important without knowing words.

The penmanship of the first anonymous letter had caught Father Tortas' attention. The letter's message had made him smile wryly. A man had written it, that much he could tell. But he knew that man was not one of his parishioners, for which one of them could write like that, express himself like that, have so little respect for him that he dared instruct him? *Hijo de puta*, he thought, what do you know, what do you know about me? Do you think that everyone can thrive in a sea of illiteracy? It had crushed him to learn that his parishioners were laborers, poor people of little education who had fled Mexico in search of something better. They defiled his language. He came to need those letters, anticipated them, counted on them to pique him, to make him think, to lift him from the drudgery of his daily life as did his weekly flights to the Loop, where he brushed elbows with his kind of people in elegant restaurants, theatres, museums. People who dressed like him, who shared his interests, who talked like him and ate like him. *Castrado*, he mused, if you had *cojones* you would show them to me, you would sign your name and show me your *mestizo* face. But you half-breeds have always been cowards. Only cowards live in the *culo* of Chicago and like it. I could find you out if I wanted, but I give your letters the importance they deserve—anonymity. You amuse me, *enano*, you faceless dwarf. Still, he wondered who his Momus might be.

As time passed, Father Tortas became convinced that his critic had to be one of the parish's heretics. Chema was his prime suspect, but without inquiry he could not learn enough about him to confirm his suspicions. In the end he abandoned all desire to ascertain who the offender was because it did not matter that he identify his anonymous correspondent. And he did not want to deter the man.

Once, several years before the priest brought out the bulletin, the two men had met. It was in the depths of *la crisis*, the Depression, and José María had been lucky to be working one and two days a week. His family was large, his children very young, and he needed additional work. They had learned to live without gas and electricity, but they could not do without food and clothing. There was always work to be done in the church and in the church's properties. Everybody knew this. Reluctantly, José María had gone to see the priest, driven to it by need and the hope of securing employment. He found Father Tortas in the sacristy.

"*¿Señor cura?*" José María said.

The priest turned to face a man in his thirties, lean and muscular, his Mexican physiognomy striking with its deepset eyes, prominent cheekbones and nose, a slight fleshiness around the mouth that drew attention away from the chin. He wore heavy work shoes, corduroy trousers, a denim shirt under a light jacket, and a wool cap pulled forward on his head. José María looked steadily into the other man's eyes.

"*Aquí se me llama padre*, around here people call me Father." The priest looked deliberately at the man's cap, as if telling him to remove it. Unruffled, José María understood but kept his hands at his sides. Then the priest asked, "*Eres una de mis ovejas?*" all the while thinking, whether you're mine or not you're a sheep.

"*Soy hombre*, I'm a man. *Vivo en este barrio*, I live in this neighborhood," he answered coldly, offended by the other's use of *tú*. Fucking priests, he thought, they're all alike.

"*¿Qué quieres?*" the priest asked, thinking, yes, you bastard, just what is it that you want?

Hijo de la chingada, Chema thought, *van dos veces*, that's twice you've done it now. Again, the answer was cold, "*No quiero nada*, I want nothing. I have come looking for work. I am a good painter, a fair plumber, a carpenter. I can repair anything that needs repairing. I am a good electrician too. Pay me what you like, *lo que quiera usted*; if you don't like my work, don't pay me anything. I need work."

"The men in this parish donate their skills to their *párroco*. Why should I hire you?"

"*Mire usted*, look," he said pointing to a wall of blistered paint above a large radiator. His "*Ahí arriba*," accompanied by an upward thrust of the head, directed the priest's eyes to a badly cracked pane of glass just below the high ceiling. "You should hire me because my work stands up to time. Because I am not afraid of height."

Father Tortas sat down but did not offer the man a chair. He caught his right trouser leg just above the knee, pulled it up gently and crossed his legs. The black tailored material hung in a long smooth fold above a polished black dress shoe. "Do you have a family?"

"*Sí*."

"Which is your church?"

"I do not have a church."

"*Lástima*. I do not hire heretics. If you want to work for

me you must attend Mass here." Waving his hands back and forth between himself and José María he added, "Bring me your heretics. When I have made Catholics of all of you and you become sheep in my fold, I may hire you."

"I do better work than your Catholics."

Impatiently, the priest stood up, crossed the room, took his black Homburg from a rack and put it on. "*¿Cómo te llamas?*" he asked, as if knowing his name would give him some power over him.

"*Julio César,*" he answered with a smile. "*Y tú cura,*" he continued, "*seguramente te llamas Torquemada.*"

"I have no time for your insolence!" Tortas reached out to smooth a cassock that hung neatly on a hanger.

"Nor I for yours. I am leaving, please feel free to put on your dress." And he laughed, turned and left.

Father Tortas' experience with two of the Rivera boys was no better. On Sundays, after Mass, they posted themselves at the doors on his church to sell papers. He had shooed them away many times and once had managed to snatch their little *semanarios*, tearing them to pieces and repulsing the boys as he might have driven money changers from his temple. But they kept coming back and he finally asked them in a threatening voice, "*¿Cómo se llama vuestro padre?*"

"*Don* José María Rivera," they answered fearlessly.

Furious, the priest shouted, "*¡Entre vosotros no hay don, como no sea don Mierda!* There isn't a *don* among you, unless it be *don* Shit!"

One of the boys answered him, saying, "*¡Para mierda, los curas!* If it's shit you have in mind, we should be talking about priests!" Chema laughed when the boys told him what had happened. Father Tortas kept distant from them after that.

When Chema's eldest son, at sixteen, found a part-time job at the Wilcox and Follet Book Company, it was the dictionaries that caught his attention. "They got dictionaries up the ass on the fourth floor!" he told his brothers. "Little ones, vest-pocket dictionaries, an' bigger'n bigger ones. The biggest are those big fat Websters with color-plates."

"Do they have 'em in Spanish?"

"Yeah! On all kinds of languages. In two languages too."

The plan took form slowly and when they had worked it out to the last detail they executed it, on a Saturday. On Sunday, when José María's youngest son brought him Father Tortas' bulletin, his other sons each brought him a dictionary, the first real gifts they had ever given him, gifts that Chema could not afford. (Three times in the air shaft, heart and hands had followed perfectly the trajectory of the falling books, three times had calculated precisely the moment at which to catch, three times had shuddered with the explosions, the grime-encrusted windows becoming banks of eyes as Chema's sons struggled to hide the books in a Boy Scout knapsack.) Chema's eyes bulged in disbelief as he fingered the three volumes: a thick, handsome *Sopena*, a *Velázquez* bilingual, and *Webster's* unabridged complete with color-plates.

Readying his table in the kitchen, his new *Sopena* at his right elbow, José María picked up the bulletin and began to read it aloud, a mocking edge in his voice:

Queridas ovejas,

I remind the Daughters of our Most Holy Virgin of Guadalupe and the Knights of the Virgin of Guadalupe . . . .

"*Ahora te chingas, cura,*" he exclaimed, "you're fucked now, priest, now you'll see who's who, *sabrás que soy tu padre, tu padre*, now you'll know once and for all who your master is! ¡*Aprende*! ¡*Aprende*! Learn! Learn!"

And José María Rivera placed his hand on his new *Sopena*.

Ricardo's War

Ricardo pulled on his coat in the lobby. Something was going on outside and he hurried through the big door of the movie theatre to see what it was. Then he heard the newsboys: "Extra! Extra! Japs bomb Pearl Harbor! War! War!" Newspapers under their arms, they barked their message over and over. Everywhere people swarmed around them and traffic slowed in the streets. The air was charged with commotion.

Alarm gripped Ricardo and he felt a deep instantaneous chill. He buttoned his coat, turned up his collar and looked fearfully into the night sky. He fought back his tears as a single thought slashed at him: *War! War! That's what they're sayin'; it's war! I'll never get home! I'm too far away, never!* He was eleven and had never left the city, had ridden in an automobile twice, and had never seen a plane up close. But he knew about war—it changed everything right away, destroyed everything in a flash. At the corner, close to panic, he boarded a streetcar.

That afternoon in the bright sun the streetcars had carried him along, swaying from side to side when they sped, making him smile because he swayed with them. He had always felt safe in streetcars, liked the feeling of independence they gave him. Now it was dark and he pressed his face to the window, searching the sky for bombers. *I'd rather see them in the daytime*, he thought, *know where they are so I can get ready*. He felt trapped in that red and yellow cage—so much glass and steel that ran along on tracks—and felt his fear grow. They flew at him from his memory, planes he had seen dropping bombs—newsreel planes that for years had been bringing the wars in Europe and Asia to everyone who went to the movies, and picture-card war planes.

When he was younger he had collected bubblegum picture cards of those far-off wars. He was thinking now of the two most terrifying cards: one, its background a burning mountain of human bodies, showed a horde of naked yellow men firing rifles at onrushing tanks and infantrymen; in the other, planes were bombing a city, buildings everywhere exploding, crumbling, frightened people fleeing in confusion. His eyes continued to search the sky. Each time they found what they were looking for, he stiffened, drew in his breath, listened and waited. But the blinking lights moved across the black sky and nothing happened. He exhaled slowly and looked around at the other riders. Their composure mocked him, appalled him, and he dried his hands on his coat.

From the streetcar everything looked unchanged. Familiar buildings stood where they always had and there were no signs of rubble. But time had slowed. This ride home had always been fast and now it was taking forever. In his mind he sped on in search of his house, and, where it should have been, he found a hole. Two transfers and a long time afterward he finally spied his house. Before the streetcar came to a full stop, its doors swung open and he jumped from it, ran across the street, pushed through the front door and hurried up the stairs, not knowing what he would find. He entered the flat. Nothing had changed. He undressed silently and went to bed.

Bombers and tanks hunted him. He was naked but did not feel cold. In the dark he ran looking for a street that would lead him out of the city. A street unknown to him. If he did not find it before dawn they would see him. They were in hot pursuit when he opened his eyes.

Monday morning. *I must be crazy*, he thought, his heart racing. It seemed no different from other mornings. He got out of bed, heard the others' voices, then he heard it on the radio. It was true! Buttoning his shirt, he tried not to listen to the radio. It terrified him with details. He plugged his ears with his hands, pressing hard, and went to the kitchen. From the table the newspaper fired its headline at him: JAPS BOMB PEARL HARBOR! His hands fell from his head, his arms dropped to his sides. The radio blared.

At school he found things exactly as he had left them on Friday. There were no barricades. No gun emplacements. No troops stationed close by to protect the children, to guard the steel mills, two short blocks away, from surprise attacks. What would they do, Ricardo wondered, against guns and bombs and tanks? What if he never saw his family again? It had happened to his mother and father—in Mexico, the Revolution. They had told him. Without warning, the machine-guns started. Children running in the streets, dropping books, caught in crossfire. Shells. Falling buildings, people inside. They came with guns, looking for food and money. Killed. At night too, when nobody expected them. And the stink of dead bodies.

Before the week was out Germany had declared war on the United States. Ricardo was struck dumb with fear.

It baffled Ricardo that they were not afraid, wounded him that they were so unfeeling, so different from him. More than anything, it shamed him, shamed him to speechlessness, separated him from them, casting him deeper into fear and shame. How could he tell them? How explain to them what they could see?—that everything was unprotected! They would laugh at him, single him out, call him names. *Coward*! He buried his head in his hands. ¡*Cobarde*! It was the worst thing his father could say of anyone. ¡*Cobarde*! What his mother called him when he struck his younger sister. ¡*Cobarde*!

There it was, his terror. He wanted to push the war away. If he didn't think of it, didn't hear or read about it, it would go away. News of defeat terrified him, and reports of victory only meant that the war went on. He would avoid it, it was the only way.

In the early months of the war, a current events class was held once a week, more often than that if the fighting was fierce. Using large maps, the teachers tracked the war for the children. They answered questions and explained why America would win: "We've never lost a war because we're the most powerful nation in the world. We've never had to fight a foreign war on our own soil. And we're the world's first democracy, the land of the free and the home of the brave." They explained how America was winning the war even when it seemed that she was not: "We've just begun to fight. Wait until we reach full production. They sneaked up on us, but things will be different now that we know what's what." Ricardo tried not to hear, thought of the park, movies he had seen, the swimming pool at the YMCA.

As if to mock Ricardo, the whole school was suddenly caught up in "the war effort." "Patriotism" became a common word and the principal, Mr. Fitts, spoke of it repeatedly in assemblies that were held often now. In the auditorium, principal, teachers and students gathered to sing songs ("God bless America," "Anchors aweigh," "Over hill, over dale, as we hit the dusty trail," "From the halls of Montezuma," "O, semper paratus," "Off we go into the wild blue yonder"), to hear stories of American bravery and heroism, to cheer the teams of students that, armed with rifles and sabres and American flags, performed crisp drills. There was no let up.

All those assemblies made Frederick Douglass Sneed important. He was as big and strong as a man and never misbehaved in class, and Mrs. Gleason, the English teacher, put him in charge of a crew of boys to set up the stage on assembly days and to put things away afterward. She said it was a job for the boys who had learned all they ever would in class, those who didn't mind straining their backs or getting dirty and would do more good in the auditorium. Freddie, who had complete control of the boys, made Ricardo his "lieutenant," and Lalo, Mario and Manny rounded out the "squad."

Calls for national cooperation, vigilance and sacrifice reached Ricardo's classrooms from the White House. His teachers, their voices like bugles, sounded the alarms that came from Washington: "Now, children, we must be careful, we must all work together. Chicago is the most important city in the entire war effort because of our steel mills and railroads. It's something the enemy knows. We must be on our guard against spies and sabotage. Look out for strangers who ask about the steel mills. Tell the police. Tell your fathers not to talk about their work to strangers. Don't repeat anything your brothers in the service say about troop movements. Remember, 'A slip of the lip might sink a ship.' "

These warnings fueled Ricardo's fears, which flamed like the fires in the steel mills, burning day and night now and filling the sky with smoke. They were things he had to know for his protection, but he didn't want to know them.

One day the windows, eyes that looked out from the numbing drudgery of the classroom, began to be blinded one by one. Ricardo watched every detail of the operation. Measurements were taken, the blades of the big shears cut cleanly, cement was applied carefully. It took time, but in the end every window was blinded with a heavy gauze-like cloth. Now everybody was protected. In an air raid nobody would be slashed by flying knives of glass. The wounded-looking windows, bandaged like casualties of the war, oppressed Ricardo. He could no longer look out; he would not see *them* when they came. He would have felt much safer with a battery of anti-aircraft guns on the playground.

The air raid drills were orderly, full of urgency and fearful excitement. At the sound of the alarm the teachers, like platoon sergeants, quickly moved the children to prearranged areas. Taking shelter in the building, they shunned its most vulnerable spots—open spaces, windows—and found cover under tables and desks, along inner walls, in the basement. For several minutes— while imaginary planes flew overhead and until the all-clear signal sounded—they all curled up on the floor. Ricardo could hear some of the others whispering:

"If they come for the mills, we'll never escape, we're too close. My father says so. They'd hit us too."

"If they come! But they won't. They can't fly that far. Across the ocean."

"They take off from carriers. It'd be easy to get here!"

"We'd shoot 'em down before they got this far!"

"Yeah! Like we did at Pearl Harbor!"

Easily stirred, Ricardo's imagination filled the skies with planes that dropped bombs on the steel mills. He curled up more tightly, pressing his hands to his ears, and waited for his bomb, knowing it would blow him to pieces when it found him. He remembered Fourth-of-July firecrackers he had set off under glass jars.

The war filled Ricardo's world. Day after day it made its way into everything, touched everybody's life. Young men over eighteen disappeared into the services, their lives represented by blue stars displayed in windows, their deaths by gold stars, and there was a lot of talk about blue-star and gold-star mothers. The dark green pack of Lucky Strike cigarettes abruptly turned white because "Lucky Strike green has gone to war." Suddenly there were more jobs than workers, and *braceros*, laborers from Mexico, appeared everywhere. In mills and factories women took over the work of men, carried lunch pails, began to drive taxicabs and trucks. Ricardo's father sometimes worked seven days a week and his older brothers found jobs. Debts of many years standing were finally paid off and, for the first time, worrylines disappeared from his mother's face. His father now kept a couple of bottles of beer in the icebox. Certain things that his mother needed became scarce or were rationed—sugar, coffee, meat, soap, paper goods. Some people bought them at high prices on the Black Market. For Ricardo's teachers it became harder to buy nylons, cigarettes, and gasoline; they did not hesitate to ask their students for ration coupons that their parents did not use. More than anywhere else, Ricardo heard the war in popular songs that filled the air: "Dear Mom, the weather today . . . all the boys in the camp"; "They're either too young or too old"; "There's a star-spangled banner waving somewhere"; "Praise the Lord and pass the ammunition"; "Comin' in on a wing an' a prayer"; "Rosie, the riveter"; "There'll be bluebirds over the White Cliffs over Dover." Ricardo, who loved the movies, seldom went now because movies about the war filled screens everywhere. Unendingly, the war dragged on.

Ricardo knew that the Japanese and the Germans were "the enemies of freedom." Everybody knew it. The Japanese even more than the Germans, because they were so sneaky. He did not know a Japanese; there were none in his school. But he knew what they looked like from newsreels and pictures in the paper. Mrs. Gleason explained that they were "just like Chinks, only smaller." Now, whenever he could, he would look through the window of the Chinese laundry a half block from the YMCA and feel that he was looking at "the enemies of freedom." Along with everybody else, Ricardo learned that the Japs were doubly yellow —they had yellow skins and they were cowards. *¡Cobardes!* Sneaks especially, that's what they were. Mrs. Gleason never tired of telling her students that "The lesson of Pearl Harbor is that those little animals can't be trusted. That's what we mean when we say, 'Remember Pearl Harbor!' We can't trust little animals anywhere in the world! It's like 'Remember the Alamo!' " And this made Ricardo very uneasy.

Japp's Potato Chips had been a part of Ricardo's life as long as he could remember. Their blue and gray waxed-paper bags hung temptingly on little stands in every store. Now suddenly they became Jay's Potato Chips. And now his older brother Ramiro called him Tojo when he got angry at him. It wasn't just that he, Ricardo, wore glasses. There was something more. "You look Japanese," Ramiro would say. "Look at your eyes, it's there. Hasn't anyone ever told you?" When he was alone, Ricardo searched his face in the mirror. And he studied Japanese faces whenever he saw them. In the end he saw that Ramiro was right; it was in his eyes—they were tipped and slightly puffy. And he was dark like some of them, had their dark eyes and black hair.

"What we gonna play?" somebody asked. It was recess and they were on the playground.

"Remember Pearl Harbor! Let's play war!"

"We need some Japs. Who's gonna be the Japs?"

Ricardo moved away slowly, hoping they wouldn't call him back. He took off his glasses and cleaned them.

"Hey Freddie, you be a Jap!"

"You crazy? I can't be no Jap, I'm colored an' big!"

"Well I can't be no damn Jap neither! My eyes ain't slanted or swolled up."

"Who's ever the Japs can win the battle!" somebody offered.

"Then you be a Jap, you're so interested!"

The bell rang, ending their quarrel.

The Germans were different. Not like the Japanese. Nobody said the Germans were sneaky. They were big, blond, blue-eyed, like many Americans; but they looked tougher. Everybody said they were smart, said their scientists were the best in the world. Only the Americans were smart enough and tough enough to beat Germany. Ricardo knew some Germans, German-Americans, had always known some because they went to his school. Ernie Krause and Olga Schmidt were in his class. Nobody said anything to Olga, she was quiet; but everybody jeered Ernie, called him Kraut, Heinie, Nazi, traitor, whenever he said, "The Germans got the best fighting force in the world. You'll see, they'll win the war." Nobody hit Ernie when he talked that way; his classmates argued with him, got angry with him the way they would have if he had cheered not his own but another school's team.

Ricardo wondered why nobody changed the names of German rye and sauerkraut. Wouldn't sabotage be easy for the Germans if they looked like Americans? And weren't they more dangerous than the Japanese if they were smarter? Someone was always willing to be a German in war games. And why didn't anyone say anything when children goose-stepped back and forth in front of Jake Bernstein's dry goods store, arms raised obliquely in front of them, palms open and down, shouting, "Heil Hitler, Heil Hitler!" until the old man, quivering with rage, came out with a broom and chased them away?

Germany made Ricardo think. He didn't want to, but he couldn't help it. The only way to understand the Germans was by accepting what others said—that even though they were wrong in what they were doing, you had to admire the Germans for opposing all Europe and beating the hell out of it. Ricardo understood the importance of force. It was what he and his schoolmates understood best. The trouble with this explanation was that it led you to conclude that Japan, which was smaller than Germany, deserved greater admiration because it had not only taken on some big countries, but had attacked the United States directly. It made no sense, what people said of the Germans and Japanese. Just as it made no sense, no sense at all, for people not to be afraid of war.

Everybody participated or wanted to participate in the war effort. People talked of how hard it was to do with less, and yet many seemed to have more. When he was finally forced to accept the reality of the war, Ricardo timidly began to think of how he might help. Some children felt themselves directly involved in the fighting every time they bought defense stamps and bonds. The teachers said everyone had to buy them. Anyone who didn't wasn't patriotic and wouldn't pass at the end of the semester. But few had money to help in this way and, in any case, they were not Ricardo and his friends. Mostly they were the *güeros*, those who looked like their teachers and had always boasted that they were the *real* Americans. Now they flaunted their patriotism in the faces of those who did not buy. Ricardo and his friends kept silent.

One day Ernie Krause made those who did not buy defense stamps and bonds feel good. In class one morning Ernie suddenly raised his hand. "What'll happen to the defense stamp an' bond money if we lose the war?" he asked. His tone was genuinely curious, his eyes inquisitively unblinking.

"That's a stupid thing to ask! How can we lose the war? They would take everything from us if we lost the war. Everyone would lose everything! Our defense stamps and bonds would be worth nothing!" Mrs. Gleason answered in a voice that had tightened, her eyes flashing with indignation.

"Suppose, just suppose. I mean, will the people who buy defense stamps an' bonds be treated worse'n the people who don't, I mean if the Germans find out who did an' who didn't?" Ernie insisted, unruffled by Mrs. Gleason's anger.

"How would I know that?" she snapped. "It's a horrible thing to ask! Shut up, shut up! Not one more word out of you! Why, that's impossible and you know it, you know it!"

Ricardo wondered if the war would ever end. Although his fear had receded, he had not learned to relax, and an adverse turn in the war would bring on old feelings. Air raid drills no longer aroused fear and uncertainty in the others. The teachers, annoyed by it all, no longer curled up on the floor with the students. One day Ricardo noticed that the cloth that covered the panes of glass in windows and doors had been pulled up in some corners. Occasionally, a clouded eye spied into an unsuspecting classroom from the corner of one of the door panes.

Toward the end of the second year of the war a scarcity of paper brought the war effort to the very door of Ricardo's school. A national call for an all-out effort to salvage cardboard and paper was aimed at school children. Ricardo's principal, Mr. Fitts, visited every classroom to explain what had to be done: "We need paper to win the war, mountains of paper! Paper for messages, paper to keep records, paper for maps, for war books and military manuals, paper to pack and ship things—food, equipment, clothing. Can we win it? Can we?"

"Yes! Yes! We can!" the children assured him, their voices ringing.

"Good! I knew I could count on you," he confided. "It'll be hard work," he added, "but we must do it, we must, for as long as it's necessary," and he clenched his fist and waved it at their enemies.

Mr. Fitts gave the children one afternoon off every two

weeks to collect cardboard, newspapers, magazines, and to bring them to school, where they would be stored until a truck arrived to haul them away. For months Mr. Fitts and his teachers had worked to cultivate love of country in the children. The success of the paper drives rested on the strength of that love and the principal wondered how deep it went.

In Ricardo's class the first drive was a very great success. Spurred by patriotic zeal and a keen sense of purpose, the children hunted their prey like new warriors eager to prove their valor. They searched basements, attics, coalsheds, garages, and by three o'clock they returned to school with great piles of paper. They came with their arms full, stopping along the way to rest; they came pulling wagons, pushing wheelbarrows and buggies, all shouting, "We'll win the war with paper! We'll win the war with paper!" They collected so much that most of them had to make several trips to get it to school. Freddie, Ricardo, Mario, Lalo and Manny worked as a team and brought more paper than anybody else. But in all the commotion, in all the coming and going, the stacking, the shouting and laughing, the working and horsing around, nobody noticed it. And nobody noticed that Ernie Krause refused to have anything to do with "all that silly shit."

It was Ricardo who realized that the area where they lived, and beyond, had become their battleground. It was he who told his four friends that what they did in the drives would be their part in the war: "It'll be like fightin', really fightin', an' not any of that stamp an' bond stuff." They had been a working crew; now they would be a fighting squad. It was the turning point in the war for Ricardo.

Freddie, narrowing his eyes and talking through his teeth, said what they all felt: "Them bastards, Walker an' Ryan an' Pelky an' their friends! Think they're so goddamn American. Think they're the only Americans aroun' here."

"We look for paper whenever we can, seven days a week. Then we store it until we pick it up drive-day," Ricardo explained to his friends after the first drive. They were in a corner of the school playground.

"Yeah, 'cause all that easy paper's gone now. Everybody got it. Everybody's gonna wanna get it an' there ain't gonna be that much," Manny added, gently moving his head in agreement. His eyes were shining with seriousness.

"We don't want nobody else comin' with us, right?" Freddie asked, the tone of exclusiveness hard in his throat.

"Right! We're a team! Only good team I ever been on. We don't need no damn *güeros* on it," spat Mario.

"While they're playin' an' screwin' aroun', we'll be fightin'. We'll be whippin' Jap ass an' Kraut ass with all that paper." Lalo's voice was steady, the words clear. He was jabbing the ground with a stick. Suddenly he laughed and said, "An' we'll be whippin' *güero* ass too!"

His voice bright with emotion, Ricardo told them, "I know where we can get a big goddamn wagon with iron wheels!"

Ricardo became their leader. He thought about where they might find paper and how they would collect and store it. "We go first to the houses with blue an' gold stars. They wanna help more'n anybody else, 'specially them blue-star an' gold-star mothers." He thought more about the whole thing than they did and he gave orders and they obeyed. Time began to slip away from him, to move forward too quickly.

It was harder to find paper for the second drive, and this discouraged many students. By the third, the fun was gone from their enterprise and grumbling became commonplace.

"Who ever heard of paper bombs?"

"Maybe they're shootin' spitballs at the Japs an' Krauts."

"We shouldda won the war long ago! Who are the Japs an' Krauts? Nobody!"

"Must be a lotta shittin' goin' on, all that paper our sides been usin'!"

120

"I'd show them Japs an' Krauts! Jus' gimme a machine-gun!"

Ricardo memorized a speech like the one Mr. Fitts had given, and he and his team went everywhere—to stores, taverns, restaurants, factories, packing houses, barbershops, beauty parlors, filling stations. Like guerrillas, they learned more with each drive, broadened the range of their operations and became more single-minded in carrying out their mission.

In Mrs. Gleason's class only Ricardo and his men brought back larger and larger piles of paper with each drive. This puzzled her. She had expected the *most American* of her pupils to collect the largest quantities of paper, the pupils who got the best grades and bought most of the defense stamps and bonds. Something was wrong in all this, she knew it.

After the third drive she had devised a system for grading the paper-collecting effort of each student. Using colored stars, she inverted the color-order assigned to grades in class work. Those who brought no paper were dishonored with a gold star ("It means you're dead"); a silver star designated those who brought a modest amount ("At least you're moving"); a blue star went to those who really did their share ("You're fighting like our boys"); a red star honored Ricardo, Freddie, Lalo, Mario and Manny ("You're our commandos, school commandos").

When Ricardo and his squad returned to school with mountains of newspapers, cardboard and magazines in their wagons, they did it proudly, confidently, stirred by the approval and disbelief of fellow students:

"Wow! Lookit that paper!"

"Damn! Where'd you guys get all that paper?"

"You been savin' it for months!"

"Boy! You guys could start your own junkyard!"

Freddie's unassuming "Shhiiit! Ain't nothin' like the paper we bringin' nex' time!" expressed exactly the feelings of his fellow commandos.

123

Now the days rushed by for Ricardo. He had put his fear behind him and followed news of the war with the keenest interest. When America or the Allies suffered a setback, he would rouse his commandos to an intense search for paper and cardboard, hoping to offset the defeat.

One afternoon Mrs. Gleason announced to her class that they no longer would take part in the drive since they were bringing in so little paper and staying out of class all afternoon. She made one exception—Ricardo and his squad. "After all," she told the others, "they're bigger and stronger than most of you and they know where to find it."

Mr. Fitts learned about the mountains of paper the five boys unfailingly delivered and he called them to his office to commend them. It forced Mrs. Gleason to get them larger red stars, and a bit later she named them the "Commando Reserves Enlisted To Increase National Strength." She entered their names on a special list with this title and displayed it prominently on the bulletin board. All this gave the boys a real sense of their worth, finally bringing them the official recognition they craved.

Then it occurred to Mrs. Gleason that the undue attention heaped on the five boys was working to the detriment of her best students. After all, they had feelings too; in fact, they were probably more sensitive. To put an end to bruised sensitivities, she bluntly addressed the class: "Now, all of you know that there's backwork and there's headwork. Let's put things in their proper perspective. Those of you who do backwork well should go on doing it, and those of us who do headwork well should get on with *it*. War turns everything upside-down. Do I make myself clear?"

Soon after this she began matter-of-factly to call Ricardo and his crew "the CRETINS," an acronym that filled them with pride. Without a single exception, their schoolmates called them "the COMMANDOS."

Jitomates

Jitomates . . . I was a student in high school when my mother gave a big jar of *jitomates* to a neighbor who was making *salsa picante* and had run short of this essential ingredient. The following day she paid my mother with a number two can and after that ran short with predictable regularity. My mother did not seem to mind parting with the jars as long as the woman brought her a number two can, but I did not like the exchange. They had been canned some years before and, even though I didn't see them every day, I knew they were in the basement, knew my mother went down for one whenever she needed it. Before they all disappeared, I salvaged the best of the big jars, keeping it on a table in my room. My brother Lázaro thought I was crazy. I could not explain to him why I wanted it, I only knew I did. It reminded me of marbles I had had as a child—spheres with spectacular frozen swirls, round glass traps that held cloud formations and stardust—and it reminded me of the silent world of inclusions I had once seen in a large amber pendant. There was something else too that drew me to it, but I did not know what it was.

The jar was moved from place to place, nudged, bumped, neglected. Sometimes it wound up on the window sill, sometimes on the bookcase. At times it was surrounded by shirts or buried under trousers. After a long time, it disappeared. I did not notice its passing. Weeks later I discovered I had lost it forever and felt vaguely disturbed. Years later, in a museum, I saw a paperweight of pale greenish-blue glass with a sun-like ball embedded in its center and I remembered my jar, thought about it obsessively for the remainder of the day. And I knew then why I had wanted to keep it all those years ago.

It was in January and February, in the dead of winter, that they seemed to me most vulnerable. The blue-green jars were still dense with them, with the big red *jitomates*, and I would go slowly down the unsteady basement stairs to the old shelves where the plump jars stood, row upon row, lift one and put an empty jar in its place. Carefully, I would mount the stairs with the naked red balls that were safe from the pressure of my grasping fingers. My mother used up our *jitomates* so regularly that they would all be gone before the new season had given us the first vine-ripened crop. They were the *cuerpo* of the *salsa picante* she prepared daily, the martyr who offered essence and color to her *arroz*, the round flesh that melded flavors in the deep pot of her *caldos*, the peacemaker in her *frijoles borrachos*. Outside of their jars they gave in to endless, dutiful transfigurations.

Maíz was not as important. My mother made *tortillas de harina*, white and tasteless to my liking. When she could she bought *tortillas de maíz*. These she could not have made; it would have been too costly and time-consuming. In the winter we kept our *mazorcas*, ears of corn gone hard, in a heap on the attic floor. There, across time, we freed the captive grains by rubbing two ears together, or by turning aggressive and pushing thumbs, which soon blistered, on the hard kernels that would serve as seed in the spring.

At the first deep frost the *jitomates* that had not been picked lost all firmness and glowed with the dark light of corruption, internal transformations having reduced their flesh to a thick liquid, as if they had been cruelly bruised. Mocking my eyes, the plants wilted, lost fluid and withered rushingly. I could see their naked arms, so recently strong and hidden by large leaves, lying stiffly on the ground. By then most of the green *jitomates* had been picked and wrapped in newspaper, where they would turn red.

My mother canned *jitomates* out-of-doors, surrounded by large pots of boiling water and legions of blue-green Ball jars and their two-piece covers. She was quite small but wielded ladles deftly, untiringly. My brothers brandished the special tongs needed to tighten the covers on the jars. Sometimes their muscle-power was discredited by the appearance of clouds of tiny air bubbles around the mouth of a jar. We helped her flay the fruit, the thin, bright skins thickly covering the ground where they lay, beside us, cast there by a downward snap of the hand.

We brought her only the finest *jitomates* for canning—large, red, firm ones, sensuously and symmetrically curved into perfect shapes that would stay with me forever. The others, those that failed to meet our standards because they were too small or too ripe or irregularly shaped, were put aside for sale or daily use. Picked and eaten at the temperature to which the sun had warmed them, they had a sweetness that surprised the mouth, accustomed to eating them cool. And picking the *jitomates* was easy since we were under no constraint to do it quickly. A twist was enough to release the ones that hung round and red against the green plants. But there was more pleasure in reaching into the plants for the hidden ones, our fingers fumbling in the thick foliage that stained our hands with its essence and hid nothing more startling than a nest of birds or a frightened young rabbit.

The potatoes were different. They ripened much later and we went at them with a fork, tentatively, afraid of damaging them, digging deep, wide circles, often finding them where we did not expect to. Our *maíz* was stately—tall green spears that shot above my head and held back the hot sun when I walked through the long rows. But it could be monstrous, for ears sometimes went mad, bursting through their green jackets with huge tumors and cancers shrouded in black velvet, belching grey matter like craniums that had exploded. Only the elemental pleasure of eating *elotes* cooked in five-gallon metal cans set on wood fires could drive from my mind's eye leprous eruptions held high in husks that split from internal pressures during the short fruiting season.

Year after year I forgot how fast the *jitomate* plants grew. Starred with yellow flowers and studded with little green balls, they had to be staked to keep them from breaking under their own weight and falling to the ground. We worked with wooden slats made into crosses of all sizes, driving them into the ground and hanging the plants on them with henequen twine. Some plants had the appearance of tiny ships, their several masts aimed at the heavens, green sails waving gently in the slow-moving air; others were like mobiles made immobile, their green arms bound by the straight lines that should have set them free.

Even before staking them we were responsible for the luxuriant growth of those plants. When it didn't rain we watered them lavishly, digging wide trenches around the base of their hilled stalks so the water would not run off. The work was not difficult; it was endless and routinely dull. We protected the plants jealously, but felt no affection for them.

In war our protectiveness was exacerbated. We waged it at intervals against green caterpillars grown fat and smooth and obsessed with devouring our plants with their restless cutting jaws. Painstaking search of the foliage revealed our enemies and we seized them by their menacing red horn, ripping them from the leaves to which they clung and depositing them in a large coffee can. Sometimes their grasp was so tenacious that leaves were torn from the plants, and our rage, thickened by curiosity, made us tear off the horn and grind the beasts underfoot, our soles unyielding to an elastic resistance that finally gave way to mounting force. Helplessly, the monsters perished, erupted, releasing a dark-green gelatinous blob veined with milky threads. We would spread out our captives in a pan, douse them with gasoline and watch them writhe in the inferno that sprang from a match. At the end of the battle only a heap of charred bodies remained, strewn among gleaming black-green clots. We viewed them with children's eyes.

There was a way in which we worked harder to cultivate the other vegetables—peas, green beans, squash, peppers, carrots, radishes, beets, *maíz*. For in the beginning the invasions of weeds would have choked off the domesticated sprouts had we not levelled the invaders repeatedly with our hoes. Later we thinned the young plants, freeing the strongest for unchallenged survival. *Cilantro* alone grew untended, flourished with little care, and we planted it in two-week waves to have a fresh supply for as long as the season allowed. We never planted flowers.

Late in April the *jitomate* plants, bedded in flat wooden boxes, were transplanted into fertile black earth. With the *maíz* and potatoes, the *jitomates* claimed most of the modest acreage we considered our property. It was land that belonged to one of the railroads, and many of the hundreds of acres that just lay there had been cleared and cultivated by other *milperos* like us. Taking them from the box-beds we brought in a big wagon, I handed the plants to my father and he set them gently into the earth as he aimed down the cord that stretched the entire length of the row. Then he firmed the earth around the roots, drawing it to them and pressing it down sharply. He did it swiftly, over and over with an economy of movement, did it in silence except for a closed-mouth "Mhhh!" that accompanied his every downward push. The rows were arrow-straight, the field, military in its bearing.

It was hard to believe that those green-sailed ships, those trapped, splendid red balls had anything to do with *jitomate* seeds. But they did, and in March that relationship became disquietingly clear. My father had saved the seeds of his best *jitomates* and put them away to await March. He had taken the richest soil he could find and we had carried it home in boxes to store in the attic next to the chimney that would be hot all winter. There, to one side of the window which filled that area with light, the bedding plants would germinate from the flat yellow seeds whose insignificance provoked my disbelief. In March we lacked only one ingredient.

It was then that my brother Lázaro and I went out into the world with our galvanized steel pails. We did it for several days, perhaps a week; to us it seemed forever. We went along the streets, near the curb, looking and picking, wanting to appear small having suddenly grown large, inciting passers-by to call out remarks:

"Hey, lookit them kids, they're collectin' hor'shit!"

"Watcha gonna do with all that, kid, eat it?"

We picked it dry, flat, prying it loose when it was stuck to the pavement. We picked it dry on the outside, moist on the inside. We picked it fresh, hand-staining wet. We picked it anywhere we saw it and as fast as we could so that our passion might end. And then we sped home through the alleys, where we sometimes found more. When it was dry, we crushed it in our hands until it became a fine dust and then kneaded it into the soil that would receive the seeds. It was my father who buried them.

One day the resurrection took place. Sprouts appeared and I thought ahead to August, when the green ships, their masts pointed heavenward, sails stretched, would come in with their full-bodied cargo—memorable, sensuous almost-spheres, firm and red, that we would flay and then imprison in blue-green jars. And I could not believe the miracle that had taken root in that dung heap.

Victor and David

And in process of time
it came to pass . . .
(Genesis 4:3)

When he was three years old, David Abelardo ran to help his older brother, Victor Cándido. Thrashing and howling, Victor struggled on the ground with Beto, who was trying to take Victor's toy gun away from him. David, arriving just as Victor lost his hold on the toy, snatched the metal gun from Beto and struck him on the head with it, drawing blood and ending the struggle. Then he gave it to Victor and the two of them turned away from the other child.

Beto's screech sent María López and Evelina Moreno rushing into the back yard where the two five-year olds had been playing together. Beto lay on the ground holding his head and screaming wildly, his face and shirt streaked with blood. In a corner of the yard the two brothers played as if nothing had happened. As Evelina watched her, María carefully wiped the blood from her son's face with the damp towel she was holding when she heard him cry out. She found superficial cuts on his head and wound the towel around it like a turban.

María flew at Victor. "¡Diablo, diablo!" she screamed at him and raised her fist. He ducked, put up his left hand to protect himself and shouted, "It was David, not me!" The revelation surprised both women.

Evelina stepped between her sons and María. "Why did you do it?" María asked David. The boy said nothing, continued playing. But Victor explained and María, frustrated and angry, grabbed her Beto by the arms and shook him so hard for starting the fight that she dislodged his turban.

Later, when Evelina told Damián what had happened, the man smiled, called David and embraced him. Victor, off to one side, watched it all silently. After that, whenever the brothers went out to play, Damián Moreno would smile and say to his younger son, "Take care of your brother." There were times when Victor questioned his parents' favoritism, but they denied it saying, "Come on, he's younger than you."

From the time David entered the first grade he and Victor left for school together twice a day, morning and afternoon. And twice a day, at noon and at three, they returned home together. One would not leave without the other, except when one or the other was sick.

Once, before the first snow had fallen—Victor was in the fifth grade, David, in the third—the boys slipped into a nearby train yard to play on the railroad cars. It was a Saturday morning. Urged by David, Victor climbed to the roof of a car and lost his footing. He fell onto the track below breaking his legs. David dragged him from the track, then went running home as fast as he could to get his father.

"He fell from up there!" David explained to his father, pointing to the car's roof high above the unconscious child. Damián lifted the child to his shoulder, the boy's legs dangling at his chest, and carried him home. David followed along chattering, holding back his stream of words only when his father interrupted to praise him for looking after Victor. When Victor regained consciousness, a little before the ambulance arrived, Evelina was beside him in a chair. Ashen with fear, she looked into his face and asked him, "What if David hadn't been with you?" He stiffened in the bed, his eyes wide, but said nothing.

One of the bones had to be reset because it did not take properly, and Victor spent the remainder of the school year at home recuperating. David missed his company terribly. He would rush home to be with him and to tell him what went on around school. Between them there were no secrets.

Along with David, Victor went back to school in September. They were now a year apart, David in the fourth grade, Victor in the fifth. Never happy in school, Victor found it difficult to return after a year away from study. He was a southpaw, a real one, his left hand a beacon that never stopped flashing, a blazing sun. When he wrote he hooked that paw, crooked it so that it seemed his fingertips were straining to touch the inside of his left wrist. It upset his teachers to see him write. They saw something sinister in it, especially when he took his place at the blackboard. "Stop that! You look like Captain Hook!" they told him, hitting him on the knuckles with a ruler. Sometimes, in the hallway, they whispered about him and pointed.

People who saw them together did not think they were brothers, but took them for friends. They did not look alike. Victor was handsome like his father, had his black curly hair and dark eyes, but Victor's skin was darker, a rich, smooth cinnamon. David was clearly Evelina's son, lighter-skinned than his brother, but not light-skinned, and not handsome. He was straight-haired, had big brown eyes and a clear voice that was full of nuances when he became excited. But he was irresistibly attractive, his person a winning configuration of traits. People saw him and liked him.

David preferred Victor's friends to his own. "It's because he wants to be with Victor," Evelina explained to her husband. But the truth was that he found them more interesting than his own and so he followed Victor and his friends around like a puppy. In time they taught him to ride a bike, to swim, to whistle with his fingers in his mouth, to sneak into the movies by looking at the posters of coming attractions and walking backwards—many things. And they taught him about girls, introduced him to "eight-pagers," pocket-sized pornographic cartoon books. He learned quickly. They laughed at his chatter and alertness. But he gradually made them forget that he was younger and there came a day when he was able to beat most of them at their own games.

"That's your last marble?" David asked.

"Yeah! Borrow me some, Dave, okay?" Pete said.

"You lost!" David pointed out. "You can't play me with my own marbles. Get some from someone else, I'll wait." Victor, who had watched them play, said nothing.

"You won all my marbles! Gimme a chance to win 'em back!"

"Don't play if you can't stand losin'!"

"I don't mind losin', jus' borrow me some marbles!"

"What's the use? I'll jus' beat you again!" David balked.

"Be fair, gimme another chance!" Pete countered.

"I beat you fair an' square! What else d'you want?"

Pete turned to Victor and said, "Tell the little shit if he wasn' so small I'd kick his ass good!"

David lunged at Pete and Victor held him back. "Do it, do it!" he said, struggling to break away from Victor. He took the marbles he had won from Pete and flung them at him. "There's your marbles, baby! Go play with the nursery kids!"

When he was alone with David, Victor asked, "Why'd you get so mad? Why'nt you let him have some marbles?"

"He's a poor loser! Cheats when he can. He don't deserve a chance. When I play him I play my way, not his."

On Sundays Evelina went to Mass with her sons. She loved Father Tortas' voice, the way it threatened, reminded, scolded, urged. Loved his Spanish, so different from hers, his lisp. She never tired of hearing his voice, even when she didn't understand what he was saying. He was so educated. Sometimes she couldn't tell if he was speaking Spanish or Latin.

132

Damián did not go with her. It wasn't that he didn't believe. After all, he prayed every night. It was that Father Tortas thought the men in the parish were not the men, fathers or husbands they should be. He said it from the pulpit. Always calling them his sheep, as if they were animals. Damián took offense at all this and did not go to Mass.

Victor would fall asleep during Mass and it embarrassed Evelina to have to wake him. "He's boring *mamá*, his voice makes me sleep, I can't help it," Victor complained of Father Tortas. Often it was easier not to take him and by the time he was twelve Victor no longer went. He stayed at home with his father, helping him with odd jobs. From spring until fall they tended their backyard vegetable garden, the two working side by side. Damián taught him all he knew and little by little Victor took over most of the work.

David's earliest memory of Father Tortas was of a robed man haranguing a crowd of silent people from up high. David saw and heard how powerful he was. The other priests were not. His mother and other sheep spoke of Father Tortas with respect, sometimes with fear. At times they whispered when they talked about him. David perceived that the man's power was in his voice, in what he said and how he said it. The priest would send forth his voice from the pulpit and it seemed to climb immediately, to soar above the heads of the parishioners and then descend suddenly, like a great bird diving.

"*Mamá*," David said one day, "I want to be like Father Tortas. I want my voice to be like his!"

"*Sí*, how proud I would be if you were a priest like him."

"Is it hard, *mamá*, to be a priest like him?"

"*Sí*. You must study in the seminary, *mucho, muchísimo*."

When he was old enough to be an altar boy David went to see Father Tortas.

"*Niño*, what do you want?" the priest asked him gruffly, but with the faintest smile in his eyes.

"To be an altar boy, *padre*," David answered.

He liked the boy at once and put him into training and he became his best altar boy—reverent, attentive, quick to master the likes and dislikes of the three priests. Every Sunday at the principal Mass David assisted Father Tortas, and it was David who got everything ready for Solemn High Masses.

"He's Father Tortas' favorite altar boy," Evelina would tell her friends. To hear her talk one would have thought that David was her only son.

Beside the priests the boy was devout and radiated an air of sweetness and intelligence. "I want to be a priest like you," he would say with passion to Father Tortas. And the man would correct him, saying, "You mean a shepherd, a shepherd!"

Victor was unmoved by David's religious fervor. "Whatta you see in that guy?" he asked his brother about the priest.

"He's a priest, not a guy!" David answered.

"Guy, priest, what's the difference?" David looked at him without answering and Victor pressed on, "Did y'ever notice he walks like an ole lady?"

"He doesn't! He walks normal!" David protested. "An' even if he did, what's that suppose' to prove?"

"You don't wanna be like him, do you? He's mean, that's what they say . . . an' they say he's a *maricón*."

"That's a lie, a buncha shit! I know him! Liars, liars! They're jealous 'cause he's so smart an' they're dumb!'

"I sure would'n wanna be like him."

"Nobody cares what you want!"

Victor couldn't believe that anyone would want to be like Tortas. You had to be blind. But then David had other blind spots. Like not being able to find his way home when he wound up in unfamiliar surroundings. Victor would tease him saying, "You get lost goin' aroun' the block."

The summer before he entered the eight grade, Victor began to have mild headaches. They lasted for hours and made him take to his bed. When he went back to school in the fall there was a small lump at the base of his head. He felt listless, drowsy, and one of his teachers scolded him for falling asleep in class. Evelina discovered that he had a slight but constant temperature and confined him to his bed. During the day, he napped and dozed, had no desire to leave the bed, lay there uncomplaining. A cold, Evelina thought, he needed rest. She would send him back to school when he was well. At night he slept soundly, except when the headaches got fierce and he moaned. He was vaguely aware of David's coming and going.

The days passed, the lump grew and Victor, who rested day and night, got worse. After examining him, the doctor said it was nothing serious, probably a lingering cold he had not shaken off because he was run-down, the lump, a knock on the head that hadn't gone down because the boy kept bumping it at night when he was asleep. He told Evelina not to worry. But the lump got bigger—the size of a cherry, a walnut, a lime. Then it got as big as a lemon and Victor was in a deep sleep most of the time, feeling only a numbness at the back of his head. Evelina took him back to the doctor, who became alarmed when he examined him. He carried the boy to his car and drove him to the hospital. The lemon, a benign tumor, was removed the following day. Victor was hospitalized for a long time.

When they finally released him he took memories of crisp white sheets, solicitous nurses, a strong antiseptic smell and vials attached to his penis. He arrived with his head heavily bandaged and a look of deep weariness in his eyes.

In the beginning David had missed Victor. But he quickly learned to get along without him. Now, seeing him with that thick bandage around his head, David felt he was looking at a stranger. "Vic," he said embracing him gently and kissing him on the cheek, "you look jus' like the movies when they first come back from the hospital."

"David," Victor said softly, examining him from head to toe and smiling weakly, "you look different."

"You too," David whispered. He had remembered a bigger Victor and now he looked smaller and frail. "Does it hurt?"

"Not anymore," he said and moved into the bedroom. David followed him. "How's school?" he asked, dropping onto the bed.

"It's okay. I been learnin' a lot," David answered, sitting down beside him on the bed. It was Victor's bed now, would be until he got well. David would sleep on the couch. "Remember Joe Maris?"

"Yeah, you mean Gumdrops, right?"

"Right, that's him. He's my best friend." He watched closely for Victor's reaction.

"When did that happen?" Victor asked, unmoved.

"Right after you went to the hospital."

"What's he like?"

"He's always got a clean handkerchief an' sometimes in class he spits in it," David said with intensity.

"I had clean handkerchiefs in the hospital, paper ones."

"You should see his house, it's really nice. His mother lets us sit in the livin' room an' talk."

"Is he smart?"

"I'm smarter," came the fast reply, "but he knows lotsa stuff. His brother's in the army an' sends him money."

"What's he do with his money?"

"Saves some, spends some. Once in a while he treats me to things. Ever have a banana split?"

"In the hospital. They're good, ain't they?"

"Ever have apple cobbler?" David pressed, eager to reveal how much he had learned.

"In the hospital. Lotsa other stuff too. Ever have any strawberry shortcake?"

136

"No," David said shaking his head. "He took me downtown to the Loop. On the train, the IC. We went to the movies, the United Artists. Ever done that?" he asked.

"No, never."

"He's teachin' me how to play cards, blackjack an' poker. When I know, I'll show you. I already know solitaire."

"You teach him anything?"

"Dominoes. He learned pretty fast."

"He called me a spic once. He ever call you that?"

"No. He calls me David or Dave, nothin' else."

"Better watch him. I would'n trust him."

"He's okay. He showed me how to play league ball an' gimme a nice mitt. It's my favorite game."

They were silent for a moment. "You tired?" David asked.

"Yeah, but not sleepy. I'm okay, don't worry."

"I never known anyone like Joe," David said. "You should see him at a fancy place like the United Artists. It's like he owns it, the way he walks right up an' asks for things."

"I seen him aroun' an' did'n notice nothin' special 'cept his gumdrops." He laughed. David didn't.

"You ain't seen him where I have. Me an' you, we'd whisper on the IC aroun' other people. He talks right up."

"Yeah? What's he say? Somethin' special?"

"It ain't what he says, it's how he acts when he says it an' where he says it. Like he's real sure of hisself."

"He like that in church?" Victor smiled.

David frowned. "Be serious, Vic. Everybody whispers in church, you know that."

"I don't."

"You don't even go to church. What I mean is Joe acts like nobody's better'n him. He don't whisper in fancy places an' he ain't nervous in places he ain't been before. Us Mexicans whisper an' we're nervous all the time." Victor said nothing and looked at him for a long time.

In April, Victor watched his father spade the back yard. Damián would not let him help, did not want him to exert himself. Nor did he let Victor, his invalid, help him with the planting. Restless, Victor knew his father had finished when he finally put in the tomatoes. But afterwards Damián neglected the garden and weeds began to invade it because he was too busy working and watching David play baseball with neighborhood teams. Habit and boredom drove Victor to weed and hoe the garden. When he saw it, Damián got angry!

"I told you not to do this, you're sick! If you aren't careful you'll be back in the hospital!"

"I'm not sick anymore, *papá.*"

"That's not what the doctor says. You disobeyed me!"

"The doctor doesn't know. Besides, the work was easy an' the weeds were takin' over. You're so busy with your job an' David's ball games."

"If the weeds take over, that's my business."

"I was jus' tryin' to help, don't be angry with me."

"I know, Victor, I know. I'm sorry, forget what I said."

In June, when David was playing ball everyday, the doctor removed Victor's bandage. Damián and David scarcely noticed. "You're all right now, Victor," the doctor said, "you can be normal again. If you get into a fight, don't worry."

Three weeks of school remained but Victor did not return to the classroom. He helped his mother with household chores and ran errands for her. One day she sent him to the store for a bottle of milk and he went to *La Milpa* for it, several blocks away. Prieto, the owner, rang up the sale and gave Victor his change. They boy counted it, held out the coins in his open hand, took a nickel and gave it to the man. "You gave me too much," he said.

The man's eyes narrowed. "What's your name, *muchacho*?"

"Victor. Victor Cándido Moreno."

"Why aren't you in school?"

"I been sick, real sick."

"Are you good at numbers?"

"I know when I get the right change," Victor said, looking right at him. Then he turned to leave.

"Wait," the man said, "Do you want to work here?"

The following day Victor began to work at *La Milpa*. He worked seven days a week, quickly learning what Prieto taught him. He sliced meat and cheese; weighed, bagged and priced beans, rice, sugar, spices; stocked shelves; filled coolers with milk and pop; dusted and swept; waited on customers. Right through the summer he worked, regained the weight he had lost during his long illness and put on a few pounds more.

Watching him one day, Prieto said, "I knew you would make a good clerk. I'm a good judge of character." He paused for a moment then asked, "Do you like my store?"

Without hesitation Victor answered, "*Sí, señor, mucho.*"

And while Victor worked, David improved his game of baseball. Fleet-footed, he gave up the infield to become an outfielder. He worked on his throwing, sharpened his hitting and when he was on base learned to keep his eye on the pitcher. If Damián was present, David's eyes would engage his father's whenever they could, a gesture that moved Damián deeply.

In the fall, on the first day of school, David left home early in the morning to meet Joe. They had to work out a lineup for a game that afternoon. At home Victor was nervous and paced the kitchen. "Relax," Evelina said to him, "you're going back to school, not the hospital."

"I can't," he said, "I'm going' to a new class an' I'll be the oldest one there." A bit later he left alone.

They were in the same class now, the eighth and final year of elementary school. David continued to play ball until after the World Series, he and Joe inseparable. "You're like twins," Evelina would say to David, not in criticism but with approval. And then, as if remembering something, she would ask, "Shouldn't you be spending more time with Victor?"

"How can I?" David asked with irritation. "He's always at the store an' I'm always playin' ball."

Now the brothers rarely left for school together. And Victor returned home for lunch but David took a lunch so that he could be with Joe. After school Victor went directly to *La Milpa*. David went to Joe's after changing his clothes.

It was hard for Victor to take up schoolwork again. He sat behind David, easily distracted by the noises in the hall, beyond the windows, but especially by thoughts of *La Milpa*, of someday owning a store like it. David, the best student in the class, sat behind Joe Maris and worked with complete concentration. But when he finished his assignments he would imagine that he was Joe's brother.

That final year of elementary school made David uneasy. His teachers seemed suddenly to remember that there was more schooling beyond the elementary level and they began to warn the students about it: "You've got a year to work on your English. Most of you will find out that you're below standard. Try speaking the way you write, it'll help you in high school." They said it so often that David heeded them. It was difficult at first to rid himself of double negatives and multiple ain'ts, but after a time he did it and there was a close correspondence between his writing and his speaking.

In the summer, after graduation, Victor and David saw little of each other—in the morning for a few minutes and again at night before going to bed. Victor worked all day at *La Milpa*. Prieto would be gone for hours, leaving the store in the boy's hands. David, with Joe, played baseball or watched it all day long. The war was fattening Damián's pay check and made it possible for David to see the White Sox play ball. Joe knew how to get to Comiskey Park on the streetcar.

That summer Evelina suffered a setback on discovering David had lost interest in the priesthood. She had seen his passion for baseball as something that would pass. Father Tortas told her. He had noticed the boy's growing disinterest months before. Evelina was caught by surprise.

"He promised me, promised Father Tortas. And now look," Evelina complained to her husband.

"He's a child," Damián explained, "and you can't hold a child to a promise. It's not fair. You know that."

"But he knows how much it means to me," she insisted.

"Let him be," he urged. He hesitated before adding, "Besides, how can any man really want to be a priest?"

"What are you saying?" she protested.

"You know what I'm saying!" After a moment he added, "We show more interest in David than in Victor. It isn't fair."

Victor's summer passed too quickly. Each night he would bring home the food Prieto gave him—overripe fruit, slow moving vegetables, cold-cut ends, dented and unlabeled canned goods, *pan de huevo*—but he no longer turned over his earnings to his mother. He bought his own clothes now and began to save money for a store. At the end of the summer he wondered if he could stand four years of high school.

Everything was different in high school. It caught David by surprise and made his head spin—all those new faces, new ways of doing things, the long halls and the winding corridor that led to the gym, all those places where he could get lost for a moment if he wasn't careful. The school swallowed up all his grade school classmates. None of them turned up in any of his classes. He and Joe didn't even have the same lunch period. Nor did their last class end at the same time.

In his English class he suffered a humiliation. Like the other students, he was called on to tell what he had done that summer. Many had gone on vacations. He never had.

"Well, I stood home all summer," he began.

"Stayed," his teacher corrected.

"What?" he asked. He did not understand her and she realized it immediately.

"Did you stay at home or stand at home?" she asked.

"Stay," he shot back at her.

"Then you mean stayed. It's the past tense of stay; stood is the past tense of stand. Do you understand?"

He nodded and slowly, carefully, went forward with his account like a soldier crossing a minefield. He felt a burning in his cheeks and a sudden hatred for the teachers who had tolerated his ain'ts and who knew how much more. When he finally sat down he swore to himself that he would never again be humiliated like that.

That first day of classes Victor got home from *La Milpa* at ten o'clock. David had just finished his homework and was getting ready for bed.

"How'd you like school?" David asked him.

"Okay, I guess," was the matter-of-fact reply.

"It's different, isn't it?" David asked wearily.

"Bigger. More kids, teachers. Did you get lost?"

"No, but I probably will tomorrow. Any kids from our school in your classes?"

"A few, 'specially in gym." His voice was flat.

"Wish you were back in grade school?" David asked softly.

"Wish I was out of school! Prieto gimme a raise today, said I'm in high school now, gettin' older."

They met at the end of the first week of classes and Joe spoke as if nothing had changed. For David, everything had.

"Why'nt you get in my shop classes? You can still change. We fool aroun' a lot, you'd like it," Joe said.

"Can't. I have to take a college prep course. You know I want to go to college," David protested.

"Eddie Duich took shop courses an' he's goin' to college. Why can't you?" Joe asked hopefully.

"Why can't you get into my Latin class?"

"With all them sissies? I got 'em in my English class an' that's enough! How can you stand that fancy sissy talk?"

"You'd be in class with me. I'm no sissy."

"You better get out now before you start talkin' like 'em."

It didn't work out for them. David couldn't see Joe on weekends, he did homework—Latin, English, Science, History.

Joe was wrong about those students. They weren't sissies. They had more than Joe, had better and they were a lot smarter. They were the best speakers of English and in class knew more about everything than anybody else. They were so confident and outspoken that they reminded David of Father Tortas. They did things collectively—participated in extracurricular activities, studied together, sang together, went to sports events together, talked about their parties and the movies they had seen. If there was anyone not able or inclined to compete with them it was David's old schoolmates. Oh, he had thought Gumdrops owned the world! Everything that had mattered to David up this point he put aside in order to concentrate on his classes, especially English and Latin.

All these concerns did not exist for Victor. The center of his productive activities was *La Milpa*. He went to school mechanically, did what was needed to squeak by, no more, often less, and made no bones about it. He didn't bother about old classmates or new ones, didn't have time to worry or care about how anyone spoke. But he was always friendly with everyone and quick to distinguish between sincerity and pretense. What mattered to him was saving a fixed sum of money each week and this he did unfailingly.

In the spring David and Joe went out for baseball. David made the second team. Joe stopped going to practice before the first scheduled game. They played David defensively in center field and used him as a pinch hitter. He did well. So caught up was he in his studies and baseball that he scarcely noticed that the war in Europe came to an end. Most of the members of the first team would graduate in June and he was sure he would be a first stringer the following year. Victor saw a game and was surprised at how well David played.

When the school year came to an end David was as good as the best student in his English class. He was the best student in Elementary Latin and as good as the best in his science and history classes. He got on easily with his classmates but kept from being close to anyone and just observed.

Damián was tending his garden alone now, as he had before his sons were born, before Victor was old enough to help him. Evelina had taken over a small corner of the yard to grow flowers. They were working together in the garden, he with his hoe, she with her shears.

"They've turned out well, thank God!" Evelina said.

"*Sí*," Damián agreed, "how time passes!" He swung the hoe deftly, cutting down weeds and hilling the earth around his plants. "What will you do when they leave?" he asked.

Evelina released a clump of carnations she had freed of encroaching weeds and it fell open, the stems radiating from where the plant was rooted, flowers held high. Touching the ground, a sinuous stem strayed from the clump and suddenly turned up, raising the plant's loveliest flower. "They won't leave, they'll always be close by, with their families."

That summer David played ball longer and harder than ever. Sponsored by local merchants, several teams were organized at Belleden Park. He tried out for the best one, the Shrikes, and made the starting line-up. Two of his Shrike teammates, just out of high school, had been his teammates on the Owens nine, the two of them first stringers. David was the youngest and least experienced player, but they made him their center fielder and lead off man and he did not disappoint them. From all of them he squeezed whatever they could teach him.

Damián worked long hours on the railroad, but whenever he could he went to the park to watch David play ball. The boy had improved so much! On deep flies to center he raced back confidently, anticipating the ball's flight, and it seemed to Damián that the field threw up no boundaries to David's prowess. Always he knew when to stop and turn to make the catch. When the ball's trajectory was flatter he ran like a wide receiver going back for a pass, his eyes uplifted as he reached high, often leaping, to make the catch over his shoulder. At the plate he was a line driver hitter, on the bases, an aggressive runner. He was all concentration while the game was being played and no longer looked toward Damián when his team was at bat. Nor did David any longer go looking for him after the game. If their eyes met, David nodded. One day Damián waited to talk to him after a game and David spoke to him in English. Realizing that his son did not want him to speak Spanish in the presence of teammates and fans, the man felt humiliated speaking broken English to the boy. After that he never went to another game.

When Victor got home at night David was asleep, and when he left in the morning David was still sleeping. They shared a bedroom and each had his own bed. He would look at David before leaving in the morning, observe the smooth, serene face, listen to the slow, measured breathing. Victor wondered what went on in that head and heart so different from his own.

What Victor wanted was financial independence. His head and heart worked to that end. He remembered the Depression years when his father stole milk from door steps. Victor admired and envied his boss, Prieto, a very dark-skinned man with thick, straight, black hair. Prieto worked hard and long but without taking orders from anyone. And now that Victor was in the store Prieto would sometimes be

14

gone half a day and longer. People kept telling Prieto to enlarge the store; he would shake his head and laugh. During the slow hours of the day he was teaching Victor to drive the panel truck and now suddenly Victor decided that he would buy a car as soon as he could. It was a life like Prieto's that Victor wanted.

She sat in front of him and at the sound of his voice she turned to look, looked suddenly away, then just as suddenly turned to look at him again. "David?" she asked in a small voice, "David Mowreeno?" It was the first day of school.

He smiled, "Yes, Elizabeth Harmon, 'David Mowreeno.' "

"I didn't recognize you at first."

"I've changed." He was a couple of inches taller than the year before and fifteen pounds heavier.

"Yes, you're so *dark*!" she said with aversion.

He felt a tightness in his chest, took a deep breath and said, "I played ball all summer. You know how . . . " He cut off his words when he realized he was apologizing. *Fuck you*! he thought, feeling painfully self-conscious.

"You're so dark!" she repeated with a shudder.

He stiffened. "I tan easy," he blurted.

"You're Mexican, aren't you?" she asked accusingly.

"Y . . . y . . . yes," he sputtered, choking with anger and hatred. He had suffered that question before, asked always in the same way, and always it took him by surprise. *You cunt*! he thought, I'm as American as you! Guys from my neighborhood died in the war defending your ass! The war with Japan had just ended and Father Tortas had asked him to assist him in a special Mass to honor the community's dead *mexicanos*. He turned away from her.

She tapped him on the shoulder to get his attention and pointed beyond the open door to a group of dark-skinned students who chattered and laughed outside the Spanish class waiting for the bell to ring. "You're like them," she said, "you should be in that class, not this one." She challenged him with a look and smiled.

He was struggling to control his rage when he said, "You belong there, this one's too tough for you." He knew she was an average student. In his chest he could feel his heart leaping wildly and he moved to another desk, afraid that he would strike her if she said anything more.

One day followed another and Victor found friends—guys like him who worked after school, guys doing time in high school, waiting to be paroled. Theirs were easy friendships that did not extend beyond school. Victor and his friends moved at the edges of school life, disdained extracurricular activities, were silent in classrooms, hell raisers when they could be. Habitually tardy, habitually remiss about homework, they waited impatiently for the high point of their school day—the lunch hour. In the lunch room they were raucous, coarse, drank shakes and malts, ate three and sometimes four hamburgers, double orders of French fries, sundaes. When one was short of money the others lent him some and at the first opportunity he paid them back. They never quarreled about money as others often did. They were too concerned with the future to worry about high school.

One night David was still doing his homework when Victor got home. "Why ain't you in bed?" Victor asked.

"Have to finish this Latin assignment for tomorrow," David answered. It was a difficult translation for which he had volunteered and he was tired, his eyes bloodshot.

"Got to bed," Victor said, "the world ain't gonna end if you don't finish. That shit'll keep." They were in the kitchen and Victor began to unbutton his shirt.

"I'm not you!" David snarled. "We're in high school

and you still talk the way you did in grade school!"

"Who gives a shit!? Everybody I talk to understands me."

"Everybody you talk to is an idiot! You and those friends of yours at lunch! They're apes! Christ! Don't you have any self-respect? Don't you ever want to learn anything? Improve yourself? You make me sick every time you say *ain't*!"

"Keep your nose outta my business!" Victor threatened, pulling off his shirt and winding it around his left hand, which he shook to emphasize his words. "I know stuff you'll never know an' it ain't Latin or baseball! I ain't gonna be no priest so I don't need no goddamn Latin! An' I don't need no punk like you tellin' me what to do! Did you ever gimme anything, or did I ever ask you for anything? I know what I want an' that's more'n I can say for you!" He turned on his heel and went into the bedroom.

Grace Barrow, a sophomore, invited David to her Halloween party. Moved by curiosity he accepted the invitation. He had never been to such a party and was eager to learn something new. Grace came from Blackwell, the best of the schools that fed Owens. She was plump, had wavy hair, big gray eyes and nicely curved brows that almost met above the bridge of her fine nose. A downy shadow above her upper lip accented her fleshy mouth. When she spoke, she smiled.

David told Victor about the party. Victor shrugged. "Aren't you interested?" David asked, hurt by his unconcern.

"Yeah, sure I am. Who invited you?"

"Grace Barrow. You know her?"

Victor smiled. "Yeah, she's that fat stuff with the whiskers, ain't she?"

David frowned. "She doesn't have whiskers, goddamnit!

Why do you have to say that about her?"

"Okay, okay, don't get a hard-on. She your stuff?" he asked, trying to keep from smiling.

"No goddamnit! She just invited me. Does that make her my stuff? Everybody jumps to the wrong conclusions!"

"Awright, awright! Can't you take a little joke? What happens at her party?"

"I don't know. That's why I'm going."

"Where's she live?"

David told him.

"Pretty fancy neighborhood," Victor said, thrusting his nose up and sucking in his lips. "Know where it is?"

"No. But how do you know?"

"Never mind, I get around." He winked. "Me an' Prieto been there. One of his wholesalers lives in that area."

"Is it easy to get to?"

"For me it is. You might get lost. Maybe I otta go too." His interest grew. "Who's gonna be there?"

"I don't know for sure, but some of those kids from Blackwell will be there."

"Glad you're goin' an' not me. Some of them bastards think their shit don't stink."

It was set back some thirty feet from the sidewalk, a handsome stuccoed house with a bank of tall narrow windows along the front. It frightened him. He checked the address on his invitation against the numbers on the house and they matched perfectly. Then he took a deep breath, walked to the door and rang the bell. A man's voice said, "Coming, coming," and then the door opened.

"Hello, I'm Grace's Dad. Come in, come in," the man said, putting out his hand. He was taller than David, very soft looking, pink and balding, his eyes gray behind bifocal lenses.

"Hello, sir, I'm David Moreno." He shook the man's hand, felt it smooth and soft in his as he stepped inside. Immediately he thought of his father's hard hands and black curly hair. The man closed the door and David's eyes swept the living room— large, carpeted, beautifully furnished. On a small table beside a wing chair, a book, a pipe, a glass with ice cubes floating in a pale liquid. The man put his hand on David's shoulder and led him through the dining room to the kitchen, where a woman turned from the stove to face them.

"Dear," the man said, "this is David Mowreeno."

She was attractive, a generously proportioned woman. "Hello, David," she greeted.

"Hello, Mrs. Barrow." David looked into her eyes.

"I'll tell Grace," the man said, moved off, put his hand to his mouth and called, "Grace, another guest!"

"Grace tells me you're an excellent student and quite a ball player," the woman said.

"I try, Mrs. Barrow," David responded.

"Do you sing, David?" Without waiting for an answer she added, "You should, you have a good voice."

Grace appeared. "Oh, thanks Dad, Mother. Hi, David. Come on, let's go down." She led him to the stairs.

There were more guests in the basement than he had expected. But it was the basement itself that surprised him. It was no dark, damp, low-ceilinged, dirty-floored dungeon— what he thought of whenever he heard the word basement. It was a large, bright, comfortably furnished room. Against the wall to one side of the stairs, a refrigerator. At the far end, the door of a well-lit room stood ajar—a toilet. And everywhere, food—bowls of potato chips, popcorn, pretzels, platters of doughnuts, brownies, hot-dogs, hamburgers, cases of pop and a punch bowl.

When the others saw David they waved and called out to him. He knew everybody there, at least by sight, and made up his mind to relax like them, to pretend familiarity with it all and to try keeping his eyes from reaching out for everything. He would be all right if he did what they did. They were eating, drifting to and away from a table heaped with food. He took a paper plate, served himself and felt better as soon as he started to eat. Halfway through his hamburger he realized he had nothing to drink and put his plate down. "I'm thirsty," he said.

"Try the apple cider, Dave" someone advised.

He went to the punch bowl and poured himself a cup. He had never tasted apple cider. He took a sip, opened his eyes wide, took a gulp and promptly served himself some more.

"Pour me some too," a voice said. It was Betty Harmon, holding out her cup.

"Hi," he said, filling the cup.

"Who'd you come with?" she asked.

"I came alone," he answered.

"No, silly," she took a sip, "I mean who's your date?"

"I don't have one." Leave me alone, he thought.

"Who asked you to the party?" She reached across her chest and tucked her left hand high under her right arm.

"Grace did," he said.

"Well, you're her date. Grace invited the girls and the girls asked the boys. You're the only boy she invited, get it?"

"Nice party," he said, making a move to leave.

"Where you going? You said you don't have a date."

"My hamburger's getting cold."

"Take a hot one, Grace won't mind." She smiled.

"I like the one I started."

He turned to go and she caught him by the wrist. "By the way," she said, "you look better already without all that color. By December you'll be back to normal and you'll look more like us." He squirmed and she laughed.

Grace led them in games and then in songs. Afterwards some of them paired off and Grace stayed beside him and he kept trying to evade her. He left when most of the others did and, like them, thanked Grace and her mother and father.

Victor was in bed, waiting. He heard David open the door and pass through the small kitchen. They lived in the back flat of the first floor; the landlady lived in front. Moving carefully, David stepped into the bedroom on his toes.

"It's okay, I'm not sleepin', turn on the light."

"What are you doing awake?" David asked. He pulled the light cord and then quickly undressed.

"Waitin' for you. How was the party?" Victor asked, blinking and narrowing his eyes, shading them with his hand.

"You should see the way those people live. Big house, beautiful furniture. How do they do it?" He turned out the light and squeezed through the narrow space to get to his bed.

For a moment a deep silence separated them. Victor bridged it with an explanation: "*No tienen el culo prieto*, that's how they do it, no sunburn on their ass!" And he burst into muffled laughter and David did too and gradually their hysteria subsided. "Anything happen?" Victor asked.

"No. Her parents were very nice."

"What about the party?"

"It was in the basement. ¡*Chingao*! It's bigger than our flat. A lot nicer too. Piles of food all over the place, like at school. You could have had ten hamburgers."

"Did you kiss whiskers?" Simultaneously the two exploded with laughter again.

There were other parties and other girls for David. He never had a date with Grace Barrow again and he never went anywhere alone with a girl, but he knew now who his friends were.

Around school it became common knowledge that David was an outstanding student. And when the baseball season got under way it became clear that he was a top-notch athlete. The first-string center fielder, he played the position gracefully. At the plate he was relaxed, rarely struck out, had a knack for getting on base—the best kind of lead off man. And he began to steal and to run bases fearlessly when Owens was ahead. Under the shirt of his uniform he wore a turtleneck jersey, keeping the collar up high under his chin, the sleeves down to his wrists. He wore it even in the hottest weather, when the sun flamed down on the players as if it would melt them, and he was composed, cooled by some inner mechanism. His cap came down on his forehead, the bill peaked to its limit, and when he took it off a band of unburned brow was clearly visible. Only his face he could not shield from the sun.

Victor ran *La Milpa* for Prieto from behind the counter. Inside there was always work to be done and Victor went out only to lower and raise the awning. But at the beginning of the summer Prieto had Victor paint the outside of the building. Bareheaded and stripped to the waist, he worked from a scaffold and his left hand quickly mastered the big brush. Watching Victor work, Prieto realized it was time to entrust him with other responsibilities. Now it was Victor who made deliveries with the truck, picked up produce at the markets, meat at the packing houses, cases and sacks at the warehouses. He would peel off his shirt whenever he could and when he returned to school in the fall he was the color of burnt chocolate. He was bigger and stronger than David.

Victor did not go back to school alone. He took along a new jeep station wagon equipped with Old-MacDonald-had-a-farm horns (David had thought the Mary-had-a-little-lamb ones were better). Damián had to sign for it because his son was still a minor. Victor had wanted something better but the waiting period for new cars was too long and he settled for the jeep wagon, a novelty vehicle that was available in two weeks.

September brought David a rest from the full summer of baseball with the Shrikes. Vigorous exercise had broadened his shoulders, deepened his chest, and he was a little taller. He returned to school sporting a thick cardigan sweater knitted to his measurements in gold and purple, Owens' colors. His letter, a big O with "Baseball" embroidered across the top, was sewn on the left above the pocket. Purple lines along the shoulders of the sweater made his shoulders look broader and three purple rings on the upper left arm identified him as a junior. Under the sweater he wore a white turtleneck jersey. He walked with his shoulders thrown back and his head held high. When he entered Mixed Chorus that first day, a class dominated by his Blackwell friends, a spontaneous cheer went up for him.

Early in the semester David was elected president of the Latin Club. He stood at the head of a small class of students in third-year Latin and was so popular with Latin students at every level that he got most of the votes. Victor, the best Spanish speaker in the school, was almost elected president of the Spanish Club. The student with the best grades in Spanish, one of David's Blackwell friends, won. Victor knew all the *mexicanos* who took Spanish, saw most of them daily in or near *La Milpa* and got along with them. He had hoped to win and would have if they had voted for him.

Around school Victor's car became all too familiar. After lunch, in the time they had left before the bell, Victor and his friends drove around the school and Old-MacDonalded the horn to the annoyance of everyone. Whenever Victor left school he played the horns defiantly, announcing that he had something more important to do than sit in a classroom.

The car made it possible for Victor and his friends to eat away from school. When the lunch lines were long or their mood rebellious they got into the car and drove off to eat somewhere else. But they liked to eat at school because they could laugh uproariously at so much that went on around them—the rivalries, conflicts, interests and pretensions of students who dove deep into the waters of high school life. And they liked to shock the students near them with what they said about classes and teachers. It was a safe, familiar place where they talked without lowering their voices.

"Raise hell an' people'll notice you. No little voice sayin' please an' shit like that's gonna do it. You gotta push an' shove if you wanna get on the streetcar. Man, it's whatcha do that's important," one of Victor's friends said.

"No, man, that ain't it! It's who you are!" another said. "Make an impression, build up your reputation, then it don't matter what happens 'cause it's your rep they think of. It's who you are that's important!"

"Bullshit! Look at me," Victor said. "I don't get on no streetcars no more, I drive. It's not what you do or who you are, it's what you got! If you got no money you're nothin' but if you got it you're king. Who you are is what you got!"

"You're all fulla crap!" another argued. "It's none of them things, it's who you know. You know the right person, he'll pull a string for you even if you ain't got beans. You know the mayor, he'll get you a good job. You know the owner of the store, he'll sell you wholesale."

"Wrong! Wrong! All of you! It's not who you know, it's who you blow!" Uproarious laughter.

Before the first snow fell Victor taught David to drive and one Saturday took David to get his driver's license. He passed the driving test but failed the written exam. He refused to believe he had failed, argued with the examiner and shouted at him. Furious, the man ordered him out, threatened to call the police. When he saw David come out, Victor knew what had happened.

"The son-of-a-bitch said I failed the written exam!"

"Wait in the car," Victor said. He returned in five minutes, got into the car and handed David his license.

"What did you say to him?" David asked in astonishment.

"Don't argue with them guys, they got you over a barrel."

"How did you get it? What did you say?"

Victor smiled and patted his wallet, "It's not what you know, it's what you got. Wanna drive the car home?" he asked.

"Sure," David answered. They got out and switched places. David, sitting behind the wheel, laughed, shook his head and asked, "How did you know you could get if from him?"

"David, are you coming to the dance tomorrow night?" Betty Harmon asked, looking him straight in the eye.

"Dance? What dance?" he said, staring her down.

"The Friday night dance, of course. They're starting up again." She crossed her arms on her chest.

"I haven't been invited. I don't know anything about it," he said without taking his eyes from her. He did not trust her and wanted to catch some give-away sign.

"No, silly, it's a school dance. Anybody can come every Friday from now on, in the gym." She rolled her eyes.

"Are you asking me for a date?" he asked, smiling.

"No, no, certainly not! Some of us plan to come and want to make sure there'll be enough guys," she explained.

"I don't know how to dance so what's the use of coming?" he said, shrugging his shoulders.

"That's no problem," she countered, "someone will teach you." For a year now she had been on her best behavior with him.

"Will you teach me?" he asked, masking a smile.

"I . . . I . . . " His words surprised her and she misunderstood him. "We'll all teach you. It's the best way to learn because we have different styles."

"Okay, you talked me into it, I'll be there," he said.

He was one of the best known members of his class, he knew it and so did they. His achievements were mounting and they needed him now as much as he needed them. They taught him to dance and he liked it so well—all the softness in his arms, the closeness—that he never missed a Friday night dance.

The better David got to know his Blackwell friends the more uneasy it made him. He had friends from other schools too, but they were like the Blackwell crowd.

"David, do you know Henry Vidal?" Betty Harmon

asked.

"Yes, but not too well. I went to grade school with him."

"What's he like?"

"I don't know him that well, we weren't close. Why?"

"He's been dancing with some of *our* girls, haven't you noticed? He's a good dancer but I think he has the wrong idea. He's been trying to date them."

"I've seen them dancing," David said. He remembered that Hank was smooth with girls but wasn't much of a student. "But I don't know what 'wrong idea' you mean."

"You know, David! He isn't one of *us*!"

"Why tell me about it?"

"The girls asked me to tell you. They thought that since you're . . . you know . . . you could tell him to stop bothering them. They don't want to hurt his feelings. God! You'd think he'd know, wouldn't you?"

"You say things better than anyone I know, *you* tell him."

The day after Betty Harmon told David about Henry Vidal some of the Blackwell boys approached him.

"Dave, why won't you talk to Henry?" one of them asked.

"I have nothing to say to Henry, that's why."

"Just tell him so that he understands," another said, "I mean Christ! Does he have to have a building fall on him?"

"Tell him yourself. You know him better than I do, you play basketball with him."

"It's not the same, Dave, and you know it. You understand him better than we do, even if you don't know him very well," a third said.

"All I understand is that it's none of my business!"

"All right, goddamnit, but don't yell at us! What did we do to you?" somebody else said.

David lowered his voice. "Let the girls tell him. It won't be the first time they turn someone down for a date."

"But David, if I were you I know I'd do it," a voice full

of sincerity said. "This is something only you can do. We wouldn't be asking you if we could do it."

"What's so special about me that only I can do it? For that matter, what's so special about you that you can't do it?"

"You understand the two of us," the sincere voice explained. "He understands you, not us. We don't understand him, he's not like us. We understand you."

"Does that make me more like you or more like him?" David asked, his eyes riveted on the earnest face before him.

"I don't know. Sometimes you're just like us, but it's hard to understand you right now. You're making too much of this thing and it isn't that important. Can't you see that?"

"You're not like Henry," another voice said, "I mean, you're a good student. You're even as good as we are."

"I'm better," David said matter-of-factly, aware that they had never before argued like this with one another.

"You get better grades, if that's what you mean."

"What do *you* mean?" David asked. "How do *you* judge?"

"We don't have to prove anything!" somebody said. "You do, that's why you're always studying. If we studied as much as you do we'd get better grades than you!"

"Let me tell you something," David said with finality, "Henry's just like you." Then he turned and left.

He felt desperately alone. Who would listen to him? And who would understand him? His parents wouldn't understand why he wanted so much or what he wanted. His mother would make a priest of him if she could! And his father had found security in a railroad section gang. Oh, they applauded and supported him, always had, but they couldn't see with his eyes. He needed more than approval! Victor was too much of a realist to understand, too practical to reach beyond the sure and narrow borders of his life. As for Joe, David had lost him. Besides, Joe was short-sighted, intolerant of education, perhaps frightened by it. But at least he didn't think he was really better than anyone else. Who was there then? His teammates? They were too caught up with baseball. And what might he expected of Henry Vidal? Henry, who had missed all the signs the Blackwell crowd had put up for him. He needed more than a sympathetic ear—he needed someone who understood all this better than he did, who had lived through it all. He had left his grade school classmates and could never go back to them. He saw them, of course, and talked to them without difficulty, but he had taken a direction different from theirs. That Blackwell crowd, they couldn't see beyond themselves! And yet, of all of them, he felt closer to the Blackwell crowd.

Victor and David were so different that many of their friends did not know they were brothers. That they shared the same last name was of no importance compared to the fact that they did not share classes, friends, activities, interests. And those who knew seemed to forget that they were brothers. Each went his way and they got along. What kept their paths from crossing was Victor's dedication to his work.

But Damián and Evelina were constantly reminded that they were brothers precisely because they were so different. And because they were different they constantly compared them. Damián and Evelina were prouder than ever of David. Every week they read something about him in the school newspaper. He was president of the Latin Club, secretary of the Honor Club, soloist in the Mixed Chorus, treasurer of the Lettermen's Club. And in the second semester of his junior year, after five consecutive semesters in the Honor Club, he was inducted into the National Honor Society, the school's most exclusive and prestigious organization.

"Why haven't you followed your brother's example, *por*

qué?'' Evelina once asked Victor.

"I'm interested in other things, *mamá*," he answered.

"Everybody talks about him, *todos*. Do you know how proud that makes me?" she continued.

"*Sí, mamá*. It makes me proud too. But can't you see how much I've done? Don't I make you proud of me?"

"*Sí, sí.* But David is doing important things, difficult things. Everybody says so."

"But, *mamá*, I'm doin' important things too! I buy my clothes an' David's! You know that even if nobody else does. I bring food! That's why you were able to buy the new furniture. I'm the only student in the whole school with a new car an' I bought it with my own money! That's important! Why can't you see that, *mamá*, why?"

Every Saturday or Sunday morning Victor would have David drive him to work and then let him take the car so that he could practice his driving. It gave him time to talk to him.

"You got a steady girl now?" Victor asked.

"No. I date a few girls, but nobody special." David shifted into third and the car purred.

"Anyone aroun' you'd like to date steady?"

"If there is, I haven't met her or seen her."

"How about Grace Barrow?" Victor smiled.

"Come on," David frowned, "I don't even date her."

"You sure liked her house an' her hamburgers."

"Not enough to make her my steady." He braked the car at a red light and Victor swayed forward, laughing.

"All the runnin' aroun' you do, you laid anyone yet?"

"Come on, be serious. No, I haven't." His tone was apologetic and offended at the same time.

"Somethin' the matter with the girls you date? Don't

they screw? Or is it you? Against your religion?"

"You screwing anyone around *La Milpa*?" David shot back.

"Nah, you know *mexicanas* don't screw 'til they're married." He winked and David smiled. "I thought you could get me a little piece if you got more'n you could handle."

David relaxed. "When I start scoring I'll cut you in."

"Do the officers of them clubs have lotta work to do?"

"No, just the secretary, with the minutes. It's easy."

He dropped Victor off at *La Milpa* and pulled away. He always drove somewhere new to familiarize himself with the city. And he always brought the car back to Victor by noon.

There was a Sunday afternoon in March when David and a group of his friends from the Mixed Chorus crowded around a newsstand, waiting for a streetcar that would take them to the director's home for a special rehearsal and a party afterwards. Somebody in the group saw it coming down the street, laughed, pointed and shouted, "Hey, get a load of this! It's the goddamned grapes of wrath!" It was a black panel truck, its underside rusting, a length of rope tied from the bumper to the hood to keep it from popping open, the sides decorated with large uneven letters that spelled LA MILPA in seven different colors. It trailed a cloud of blue smoke. Except for David, who recognized the truck, driver and rider and turned away, all went to the curb to watch it pass.

"Probably drove it right out of a junk yard!"

"Christ! Think they've ever washed it?"

"You couldn't give me that goddamned thing!"

"Who'd want to drive it? God!"

"That's who! It makes sense, they look just like it!"

Victor was driving. He saw David turn away and scanned

the group, recognizing most of them. As the truck neared the group, Prieto rolled down the widow and spat in their direction. The boys responded with obscene gestures and catcalls.

"Hey!" one of them said, "that guy goes to Owens!"

They were seconds of anguish for David. Skin color meant nothing, he told himself. God gave it no importance. Ah, but it did mean something! It meant a great deal, day in and day out, here and now! Oh, if only Victor had his ambition! He knew that he, David, had no more intelligence than other *mexicanos*. But he had so much more ambition! If Victor had his ambition, if the two of them had gone the same way together, together they would have turned Owens upside down. Keenly now he felt something cut him away from Victor, making them strangers, and just as keenly he heard his blood cry out. And in that moment he knew that they were brothers forever. Nothing could change that. Whatever happened, Victor would be bound to him, darkly, always.

David was studying when Victor got home.

"What was that shit that happened this afternoon?" Victor asked in a rush.

"What are you talking about?"

"You know what I'm talkin' about, don't play dumb!"

"Don't bother me! Can't you see I'm working?"

Victor balled up his left hand and shook it at him. "You saw me with Prieto an' looked the other way!"

"You're crazy! I don't know what you're talking about!"

"You're lyin'! You're the only one who did'n look at us an' laugh. You turned away! Why? I wanna know why!"

Evelina heard the angry voices and went to their room. "*¿Qué pasa?*" she asked.

"It's about school," David said, "it's nothing." She left.

"Why?" Victor asked again.

"I didn't see you, I was looking at a magazine." His voice lacked conviction.

"I'll tell you why! You were ashamed of me, ashamed of

Prieto an' his truck! Right? You an' your fancy friends behavin' like a buncha babies! An' you're all suppose' to be so smart! Buncha shitheads, that's what you are!"

David exploded, "Yes! You're right! That goddamned truck looks like something that belongs to a nut, like something that escaped from a junk yard! Can't the son-of-a-bitch do something about it, or does he like being a clown?"

"Lemme tell you about that clown. He treats me right, always has. Pays me the money that bought your sweater, pays me the money that bought my car, gives me the food you stuff down your throat in this house. Now if that's bein' a clown I wanna be a clown jus' like him, you asshole!"

"Why can't he wash that crappy truck and fix the hood? Then he wouldn't need that goddamned rope! And while he's at it, he might try washing his face!"

"An' I might try washin' mine too, right? Well that's the color of his face an' this is the color of mine," Victor hissed, thrusting his face into David's. "He was born with his an' I was born with mine an' all the washin' in the world ain't gonna change it one damn bit! Wash his face! You ass! Why'nt you tell your fancy friends to wash their crappy gym clothes? Think I ain't seen 'em an' smelled 'em? Prieto don't bother no one an' he don't laugh at no one an' he don't make an ass of hisself like that buncha shitheads you run aroun' with! Don't you see that, David, don't you? You're suppose' to be smart!" Victor's eyes were inflamed.

"You don't understand," David quietly protested. "I was afraid they'd think Prieto was related to us."

"Yeah, an' afraid they'd think the truck was our first cousin! I understan'! If they thought he was your relative all you hadda do was tell 'em he wasn't. It's that simple. I seen some of your fancy friends with some ugly bastards an' I did'n jump to no conclusions about them bein' relatives. You're the one who don't understand! Your high-class friends don't like dark meat an' nobody, not even you, is gonna change that." Victor made a motion to leave, paused, and spat the last words, "You an' your goddamn turtlenecks!"

David leaped from his chair and lashed at him with his fist, a blow that Victor deflected with his forearm. But it grazed his chin. Victor turned and walked away. From that day forward David took care to steer clear of Victor and to be cautious of what he did with his friends.

Long before the baseball season arrived David began to exercise—he jumped rope, lifted weights, ran sprints, did chin-ups, calisthenics. He would be in good shape before the first practice. This year he was sure he could make the all-city team. And if Owens took the sectional championship he would have a chance to make the all-state team. To win an athletic scholarship to a good college his junior and senior years would have to be outstanding. He knew that with his grades he was a better prospect than many players.

Weeks of hard work got him off to a fast start when the season opened. Early on he perfected his sliding technique and finally learned to get a jump on the battery. A runner who accelerated swiftly, he began stealing bases at will, taking advantage of every opportunity to run. His hitting was so consistent, line drives to all fields, that the coach dropped him to third place in the batting order. All his competitive juices surged with men on base; he was dangerous in the clutch.

Crowds of Owens students turned out to watch him play and this quickened his urge to win. Cheers went up when he came to the plate, got a hit, drove in a run, stole a base. Or when he snatched extra-base hits from the opposition with circus catches in the outfield, when his strong arm threw someone out at third or the plate. He played with a smile on his face.

Midway through the season, on a Friday, Owens played Lake Shore High School, arch-rival and one of the toughest teams, at Lake Shore. In the last inning, with the score tied and one out, David lined a single to right, stole second and came all the way home on a single to center. It was the only run Owens scored. Lake Shore loaded the bases with two out and the game ended when David pulled down a fly on a dead run in deep center.

After the shouting and backslapping, David went to the bench for his grip with its extra pair of spikes and spare glove. There somebody approached him and he turned to find a girl about his age. Her long hair, the color of a robin's breast, brought into sharp relief her face, a ruddy oval set with fern-green eyes, a nose delicately curved downward and a small, full mouth. She stood erect, her hands held behind her. A short way off her friends waited for her.

"Hi," she said, "I'm Edyn Agness. I just wanted to tell you that was some game. I play softball. Guess I shouldn't be talking to you after what you did. I go to Lake Shore."

He smiled and said, "I'm David Mowreeno, Edyn. Sorry about your team. Maybe you should transfer to Owens."

"You play ball as well as you sing. I heard you at the Spring Music Festival." She brought her arms to her sides and moved closer to him. "You're better than Frank Sinatra."

He fidgeted with the zipper and said, "Edyn, I'd sing for you any day of the week."

She smiled. "We all liked your voice," she added.

"We?" he said with curiosity, eager for an explanation.

"Yes, the chorus and our director. You were great."

The players were heading for the gym. Some of them stayed back, motioning him to join them. He waved them on. "They're waiting for me," he said.

She stepped back saying, "I wanted you to know I enjoyed your singing and playing. We need you at Lake Shore."

She raised an arm to her friends, a sign that she was coming.

David felt an urge to touch her. She had been attracted to something in him and if he didn't speak she would leave and he would never see her again. If he was wrong and she rebuffed him he could bear it. He realized for the first time that he had never given a girl the opportunity to reject him. There was no awkwardness in the silence that followed, only a sense of expectancy, as if both were waiting for some imminence to occur and wanted to give it a moment.

Then a sudden chill lanced David's breast, his fingertips went cold and he said, "Edyn," his voice rising on the second syllable, "you don't know me but could we do something tonight if you don't have any plans?" He was fumbling with his grip now, stuffing his glove and sunglasses into it.

She smiled and the tip of her nose moved. "I'm free tonight. If it's all right with you, why don't we come to the Lake Shore dance. I'll meet you in front of the gym," she turned to point, "there, at eight-thirty."

Then David went up to her, took her hand and pressed it softly. Turning to go he said, "The guys will wonder what's up. I'll see you tonight." And he ran to catch up with them.

They fell in love, Edyn and David, the two bubbling over with talk and energy. She was an excellent student, enthusiastically involved in extracurricular activities. He met her parents and liked them. Mr. Agness was a professor of English at Wilson Junior College, Mrs. Agness, the proprietress of a boutique on 71st Street, not far from the Lake Shore Country Club. And they liked him.

David did not see Edyn during the week except when there was something special. Nor did he regularly call her on the phone since the Morenos did not have one. Sometimes, however, when he found himself near a phone booth, he would call her. Edyn wanted it this way too. For David it was better than having Edyn at Owens. She would have been too great a distraction there, would have learned too much about him there.

He met Edyn's friends at parties and Lake Shore dances, found some of them more knowledgeable about everything than his Blackwell friends. And some of them seemed to have more money than his friends. But they were alike in other ways—their penchant for group singing, basement parties, dancing, the movies. What David steadfastly resisted was Edyn's desire to meet his friends, her curiosity about them.

Victor knew David was in love. He spoke less and less of his Blackwell friends and more and more of Edyn's. It pleased Victor. And because he knew the Lake Shore area and something about the people who lived there, Victor began to lend his car to David and to give him an allowance, making it easier for him to be with Edyn. It took David by surprise. Victor began to live vicariously, to move beyond the confines of *La Milpa*, where he knew he could never be as free as David. He could never force David to do what he, Victor, knew was right. David did what he wanted, even when Victor disagreed with him. But for now Victor wanted to stand with him, to give him money and a car because they were the only things he possessed that could command respect and buy some measure of freedom, to let him know he admired him for all he had accomplished, for having beaten these *güeros* at their own contest, games, competitions, just as he had done it to Victor's friends when he was a child who tagged along behind them. And David took confidence from his brother's generosity and began to ask for the car when something special came up, and Victor heard him with compassion and lent it to him, giving him gas money.

On the first Sunday in June Victor was in *La Milpa* filling a cooler with pop. He worked rapidly, grabbing several warm bottles in each hand and submerging them in the near freezing water. He had almost finished when one of the bottles exploded in his left hand as he plunged it into the water. Instantly the water turned red, and old words, leaping across years, flashed in his memory: "What if David hadn't been with you?" Victor pulled his hand out and saw the gash through the thick rush of blood. In the scarlet water he tried to wash away the blood but could not stanch the flow. Then he tore off his apron and wound it tightly around his hand. Prieto was beside him now, led him out to the truck and sped him to the hospital. The deep slash, running from the back of his thumb across to the fleshy mound just below the second joint, had reached the white bone. They watched the doctor stitch it up.

Two weeks later, on a Saturday, Victor went to the doctor's office. It was on the corner of 76th Street, a block and a half from the lake. The doctor removed the stitches and Victor left to return to work. He leaned against the building and waited. He could catch his streetcar there just before it crossed the IC tracks and it would leave him two block from *La Milpa*. He looked at his watch. It was almost four. David had his car. He had lent it to him that morning, after David drove him to work, because David wanted to see a North Side team play an important game. Edyn was with him. Afterwards they were going to a picnic in Jackson Park. He had lent him the car for the day.

In the moving car Victor saw the girl's red hair; she was facing the driver and had her back to him. He did not know it was his car until she moved and he saw David. He dashed to the curb to wave and the car accelerated. He threw up his left arm and shouted, "David!" The girl turned in the seat and the car sped on, followed by a line of vehicles.

Victor got home before eleven that night. Evelina and Damián were already asleep. At eleven he went to bed. The day had been too long. David was still out.

"David, David," Victor called softly the following morning. He took David's arm and shook it gently. "David, get up, it's six. Do you still wanna go?" David opened his eyes, blinked, yawned and got out of bed.

They left fifteen minutes later, Victor with a mitt and a grip full of balls, David with a bat in one hand, an orange in the other and a pair of spikes slung on his shoulder. They put everything in the open space behind the back seat and got in. Victor started the car up, put it in gear and drove off. David opened the window, sat back and began peeling the orange.

"The ball field in Belleden Park, right?" Victor asked.

"Right," David answered through the orange.

Victor drove in silence. Saturday had emptied him and he did not yet know what to do to David. He could wait, he was in no hurry. He had nothing to say now.

David shifted in the seat, uncomfortable with the silence. The car slowed at an intersection and David cleared his throat. "Are you angry about yesterday?" he asked, his voice subdued.

And Victor talked with David his brother, "Angry? Why should I be angry?"

"What I did, what I did yesterday."

Victor glanced at him then turned his eyes back on the road. "What'd you do yesterday?" His voice was tight.

"You know what I did! You saw me! But you don't know why I did it!" He spoke in a quick angry voice.

"Then tell me, goddamnit, so I'll know!" Victor roared.

"I couldn't stop, I couldn't," he said apologetically.

"I thought I could get a ride. But at least wave to me when you drive by in my car!"

"I couldn't stop," he repeated.

"You coulda waved!"

"She doesn't know we're brothers."

"What?" Victor paused. "Then who's she think I am?"

"She doesn't even know about you," he said quietly.

"You're crazy, you don't make no sense." He ran his left hand through his hair.

"I told her I live with a bachelor uncle. She thinks I take care of myself, do my own cooking and washing. Thinks my parents are dead." He spoke as if he were at last protesting a long standing injustice.

For a moment Victor forgot where he was going and drove on where he should have turned left. There were no cars at the intersection and he swung into a wide U-turn. He shot his voice at David, "It's like we're dead! Me, Ma, Pa, dead!"

"They'd understand if I told them," he said.

"They'd understan' anything you told 'em!"

Victor pulled the car beside a tree and parked it. The field stretched away before them.

"I would lose her if she knew. I told her I'm Portuguese. You understand, don't you, Victor? I'm entitled to what I have! I'm entitled to everything they have and I'll get it!" He was crying impassioned, anguished tears. "I'm tired of being Mexican! It's a dirty word, everybody knows it! I'm tired of having to apologize for how I look. I'm tired of being confused with those lazy bastards around me who don't give a shit! I'm tired of always having to prove myself!"

Victor turned to look at David. "Don't explain nothin' to me, I ain't your keeper! You ain't changed from when you was a kid. You still get lost. Got no sense of direction. I give you my money . . . I give you my car. If you asked me I woulda gave you my fuckin' life. An' you treat me like shit! Worse'n shit! You're as bad as they are."

David opened the door and got out. He took his spikes and sat on the ground to put them on. Victor moved from behind the wheel, rose up and stood over David. Except for them there was nobody in the park.

"You still wanna do this?" Victor asked.

"Yes!" came the answer.

Victor reached for the mitt, balls and the bat. He knew now what he must do. He handed the bat to David and together they walked to the batter's cage. For a couple of minutes he waited there, watching David pump his legs, flex his arms, swing the bat as hard as he would at pitched balls. Then he went toward the pitcher's mound carrying the mitt and balls. He bent over and unzipped the bag, slipped the mitt onto his right hand and took up a ball in his left. He straightened up and faced David, surprised at how high the mound was. Victor's shadow stretched toward the base path behind him.

"Okay," David said, "I'm ready," and stepped into the batter's box. "Throw as close to me as you can and as hard as you can. And move the ball around. Get it near my knees and work your way up to my chest and my head. Don't be afraid." He dug into the box, pulled down the bill of his cap, raised the bat and swung it back and forth, then cocked it.

Victor wound up and threw. The ball was outside and low and David didn't even move. "Come on, get it closer and higher!" David called out.

Victor reached down for another ball, looked up and saw David ready at the plate, swinging the bat confidently, feet close together, his slender shadow falling forward toward the mound. Again he wound up, reared back and threw. It came in harder and high and closer to the plate.

"That's it!"

He kept getting better with each pitch, taking his time, loosening up more and more, throwing harder and harder and he surprised David with his speed. Twice David pulled his head back, drew in his chest several times, his arms held up high, but not once did he have to step out of the box.

"Move me away from the plate, damnit! We might as well not be here if that's all you can do!" His voice was harsh and commanding and full of impatience.

He threw in close and hard, down around his knees and

David jumped back easily. Again he threw, harder still and rocked him back on his heels, the bat on his shoulder. He aimed for his chest, right where the letters said Owens and threw the fastest ball he had pitched. David shifted his weight to his left foot, pulling it back and away toward the base line, flicked his wrists and lined a shot that whistled right past Victor's head.

"Goddamnit!" he yelled, rushing the plate, "You said you weren't gonna do that!" His voice quivered with fear and anger. "That's all I need!"

David laughed. "I won't do it again, I promise. I just wanted to show you what I can do to a pitch like that. Pitch me tight, but handcuff me! Move me away from the plate and don't give me anything I can hit."

Victor gathered the balls around the batter's cage and went back to the mound thinking it's all a joke to him, don't give a shit who he hurts, me, Ma, Pa. He threw harder than before and David hit the dirt.

"Now you're pitching!" he shouted from the plate, dusting himself off. He was laughing as he dug into the box.

Victor brushed him back with four hard pitches thrown with the same unhurried rhythm of a full wind-up. Now he sped up his delivery and threw as hard as he could at the small, high target, catching him off guard, David's attention fleetingly deflected by the flash of a robin's breast in the morning sun. The ball crashed against his left temple and he shrieked, fell writhing onto the field, his hands clutching his head, his legs jerking spasmodically.

Victor panicked, stood transfixed on the mound, speechless. Then suddenly he screamed, "David!" lurched toward him and saw that he was unconscious, his temple shattered. He got to his car and drove it onto the field, beside him. Three times he tried to pick him up, three times fell to the ground with him. He lifted him into the car at last and sped him to the hospital.

At the desk he told them what had happened. A doctor rushed to the parking lot with two orderlies and Victor watched them wheel David in on a stretcher. He sat down in the waiting room. How and what would he tell his parents? After a time he looked at his watch. Prieto would wonder where he was. From the phone booth he called him.

Just before twelve the doctor informed him that David was dead. Victor shook his head. In his throat he could feel something cutting furrows. Silently he made his way to his car, got in, started it and drove east to the lake.

Father Palomo

(For Mary-Alice)

The women in his parish most devoted to him, twelve of them, had come to see him off. Each brought what food she could. It had taken them months to raise a little money and they did not know what awaited him, nor did he.

"*Padre, tamales de zarzamora*," the woman said, stepping forward with a small packet. "I know how much you like them." The man took it. "*Gracias, hija*," he said and slipped it into the *mochila* that hung from his shoulder—the kind that *campesinos* are never without—the *mochila* he had taken to carrying when he became their priest. He thought of the *tamales* the woman had just given him, purple, lustrous, imagined their delicate blackberry flavor. The Indians made them. In a recurring dream he celebrated Mass with *tamales de zarzamora*. When he elevated the Eucharist it became a purple sun raining its color down on him. And when he put it in his mouth its sweetness coursed through him and he felt a rush of vertigo and then his fingertips generated purple discs, small and thick and lustrous, and he placed them on the tongue of the communicants and he could not tell them apart, the Indians from the non-Indians. Once it happened to him when he had gone without sleep for three days, not in a dream but for real, late one Friday evening when he was saying a special Mass for these very women. He patted the *tamales* at his side; he had not eaten one in a long time.

Shyly, the others came forward now, offerings in their hands: coarse wheat patties, *chicharrones*, tomatoes, *aguacates*, limes, *chiles*, a baked sweet potato, a mango, oranges, bananas, a bottle of lemonade. By turns each placed her gift in his *mochila*, and to each he said, *"Gracias, hija."* They, *"Por nada, padre."*

Some barefoot, some in *huaraches*, they dressed as their mothers had, and before them, their grandmothers—in full, heavy, faded skirts that touched their feet; in dark, frayed *rebozos* that wound around their backs and shoulders, outlined their faces, covered their naked arms. They looked at their spiritual leader, *padre* Manuel Palomo, their eyes deep with hope and worry.

He stood waiting with them, spare and straight on sandaled feet so small and narrow that his parishioners, ancient lovers of birds, had noticed them when he came to La Huacana years ago to be their priest. "Only birds walk that nimbly," they had said. "The way he moves, you'd think his bones were hollow." He was wearing the black suit, shiny now, that he had first worn as a seminarian, a dusty-looking black shirt, at his throat a white collar. He dressed like this only when he had to; his flock distrusted men in suits. The dark gold of a straw hat ringed his head, the hat his parishioners had given him when he was new to them. "Beautiful, very beautiful. I have never seen one as beautiful," he had said, donning the broad-brimmed high-crowned hat so that they, who prized fine hats, would know he had understood the significance of their gift. Then, the hat had been almost white. He ran a hand over his face, an old habit of a man who had to shave twice a day.

In a flaking leather valise he had everything he needed for the trip: cassock, two shirts, underwear, socks, a swimsuit and his shaving gear. Passport and money he carried in a flat leather pouch strapped to his body. He would take the second-class bus to Uruapan and from there go north first-class through León, San Luis Potosí, up to Monterrey and on to the border at Nuevo Laredo. From there he would still have a long way to go.

A vehicle backfired and they turned to see a bus lumbering toward them in the distance, bright red in the morning sun. It roared, backfired again, and purred uncertainly, dragging a curtain of blue flames. Two men rode on the outside, one clinging to the ladder at the back, the other seated on the rack fixed to the roof, his body swaying to the bus' every movement. Quickly, Father Palomo whirled to face the women. He held them in his gaze for a long moment, and then the dark dove of his hand alighted on the twelve heads and his thumb traced the sign of the cross on each forehead as he whispered to each, "*Benedicat te omnipotens Deus, Pater et Filius et Spiritus Sanctus*."

"*Padre*, we'll take care of things until you return," one of them said. "My nephew comes tomorrow for a month. He'll say Mass for us."

"Pray for me. Pray that all goes well for us, that I can find a way to do what I must."

"We never stop praying for you, *padre*, or for us."

"*Padre*," another advised, "eat when you get on the bus. The food is still warm."

"I will," he said, nodding his head.

The bus stopped and he got on. Only their voices moved, reached out to embrace him, "*Vaya con Dios, padre, vaya con Dios*." He turned toward them and made the sign of the cross, the blade of his right hand rending the thin morning air. They lowered their heads.

The door closed. With a roar the bus started up again. He steadied himself. A hen clucked. He handed the driver a bill. Deftly, the man folded it lengthwise, looped it onto his middle finger, fished coins from his shirtpocket, steering with one hand and then with his elbows as he counted the coins. He fished for more and dropped them into the priest's cupped palm. The priest held his valise high, making his way to the back, nodding and greeting as he went, stepping over a lamb, a bleating kid, a knot of chickens bound together at the legs, an assortment of sacks and bundles. He sat down next to a window and took off his hat.

A voice full of anger and fear cried out from the rear, "¡*Padre*! ¡*Padre*! Bless me, come and bless me, *por Dios*!" Father Palomo rose and went to the man. Deep wrinkles scarred the man's forehead, his mouth, the large sockets around the gnarled orbs of his eyes, which were overgrown with cataracts thick like calluses. A small boy with a guitar accompanied him. "¡*Padre*!" he cried out again.

"What is it, *hijo*, what troubles you?" the priest asked, placing his hand on the man's shoulder.

"Not my shoulder, *padre*, my eyes, my eyes!" the man bellowed, flailing his arms.

The priest's words sobered the man. "Control yourself, *hijo*, you're frightening those around you." With his left hand he lifted the blind man's chin, removed his hat with his right and gave it to the boy, then placed his hand on the man's head. The calloused orbs spun wildly in their sockets, trying desperately to perceive something, and the man shook violently. "Be strong, *hijo*, take hold of yourself." Gently now the priest closed the man's eyes with his fingertips, massaged the fitful eyelids and, as he whispered, traced a small cross on them with his thumb. The eyelids quivered for a moment and the orbs beneath them rested. The man was completely calm. Father Palomo pressed two large coins into the man's hand and went back to his seat.

A guitar hummed. Serenely the blind man called out, "*Padre*, I'm a musician. I want to sing for you." A hush spread through the bus. "The song, it's . . . you'll see." He sang of love and resignation, his voice growing stronger with each note, and played the guitar with skill.

When they left the town behind and the bus began to gain speed, Father Palomo drew his pocketknife and reached into his *mochila*. He sliced a tomato, a *chile* and an *aguacate*, slit an opening in a wheatcake, filled it, pierced a lime and squeezed it into the opening and then ate slowly.

Along the way they stopped for a woman with six small children. Thick-bodied, she carried the youngest child in her left arm, in her right, a bundle of straw mats. The passengers shifted, removed belongings from seats, drew themselves in as the woman, surrounded by the children, turned toward them. She dropped into a seat near the front and the children swarmed around, clutching her. "Find a place to sit!" she said, directing them to the back of the bus.

The eldest led the way and the others followed, pressing in on him. He paused beside Father Palomo, drawn by the priest's moving jaws, then he sat down and his brothers closed in on him. Barefoot, dirty, silent, they watched the priest's mouth, their liquid eyes wide, dark, tenaciously focused. "What are your names?" the priest asked. They drew back, said nothing. He opened his *mochila* and took out some food. "Come, I'll fix something to eat for you," he said. They stood mute, staring, fearful, and when he held out the food they snatched it from him and devoured it. He gave them everything except the *tamales de zarzamora*, and what they did not eat one of them took to their mother. They gulped down the lemonade and kept the empty bottle.

Now the priest regressed almost thirty years, to the time just after his father died. He saw his mother, his brothers, himself. At once he realized what he had done and ran his hand across his face to soothe the sudden burning. He took out the packet, opened it on his knees and laid out the *tamales de zarzamora*. The children nudged one another, exchanging rapid glances. "Eat this slowly," he instructed, "understand?" They nodded. He broke the *tamales* into pieces. "Stick out your tongue," he said, "and suck, don't chew." The sucking brought smiles to their faces. When there were five pieces left, the priest closed his eyes and whispered. Then, whispering still, he made a sign of the cross with the purple fragments before placing them on the outstretched tongues. He slipped the *mochila* into his valise and for the remainder of the trip—four days and three nights—he ate nothing.

In Gary Father Palomo ended his fast at the apartment of the man who met him uneasily at the bus station. They ate *huevos revueltos, tortillas, frijoles refritos* and drank *canela* made with slivers of cinnamon. The man spoke little and averted his eyes. He was related to one of Father Palomo's parishioners. Tactfully, his voice reassuring the man, the priest gradually drew him out in conversation and discovered that he had made a mistake in coming to Gary. The man had not really believed the priest would come. His reports of opportunities and easy money were exaggerations meant to impress relatives and friends in Mexico—he was a dishwasher in a restaurant. Nor was Gary—devoid of fountains, *plazas, paseos*—the city the priest had imagined. And this man's English was so limited that he could not serve him as translator. The priest had lived too long with adversity to despair. Besides, he knew that Chicago was close by; somehow he would get there. In Gary there was no need for his talent. Knowing his host's circumstances, the priest ate little.

Within three days of Father Palomo's arrival a man of indeterminate age visited him. His eyes were clear, direct, and he spoke Spanish with a faint *gringo* accent. "*Padre*," he said, "my name is Gabriel Alas. I've come to talk to you."

"Gabriel Alas?" the priest said. "Look, it's hotter in here than it is out there, but come in." He opened the screen door and the man glided over the threshold. "How different from Mexico!" the priest continued, "All these wood houses, they can't keep the heat out."

"*Padre*, you're losing time here," the man said. "Poor Evaristo, how he regrets writing what he did. I know him from the restaurant. I eat there."

"I'm grateful to him for taking me in, and sorry that my coming has upset him."

"He was trying to save face, *padre*. Poor people in Mexico think everyone here is rich. He told me about you, told me why you've come. I promised him I would talk to you."

The priest looked intently at the man. "Can you help me? I mean . . . can you advise me? I don't speak English, as you must know, and Evaristo, well . . . that's why you're here."

They were standing just inside the door in a small room with a threadbare studio couch and a pair of shabby chairs. The priest extended his arm, inviting Gabriel to sit.

"I have just returned from Chicago," Gabriel said, settling into a chair. "I grew up there. Go to Chicago, *padre*."

"What could Chicago have for me aside from gangsters and slaughterhouses?" He smiled and sat down.

Gabriel laughed. His teeth were like knernels of white corn. "This is 1955, *padre*, the gangsters are gone. Only outsiders think gangsters still drive down the streets of Chicago with machine-guns. To us it seems incredible that strangers really believe it."

"Perhaps it's wishful thinking. Danger makes life more exciting—a priest hears that in the confessional. As long as the danger is bearable. Believe me, I have thought of those gangsters with a certain fascination. I imagine that I meet them and make them renounce a life of crime."

"Life is difficult in Chicago, *padre*. It wears priests out if they aren't strong." Now he fixed his eyes on the priest's. "What has life done to you, *padre*?" he asked.

"It had made me an instrument," Father Palomo replied without hesitation. "But Chicago, tell me about it."

"Chicago is steel mills and railroads and factories. The slaughterhouses arrived on rails. People in Chicago work hard. They like to relax when they can, to be entertained.

They love spectacles—shows, parades, ball games, anything interesting."

"Then you think I can find something in Chicago?"

"Look, *padre*, they're building a seaway to the Atlantic along the Great Lakes and the St. Lawrence River—they call it the St. Lawrence Seaway. Chicago businessmen think Chicago will be the principal port on that seaway. They say it'll be a major international port with ocean-going vessels docking in it. Money will pour into the city. The Chicago Chamber of Commerce has already begun to publicize the importance of the seaway. They've sailed an ocean-sized ship right into the city and docked it at Navy Pier, on Lake Michigan, a couple of blocks from downtown Chicago. They christened it the *Aquarama* and are saying it's a harbinger of ships to come. It's a floating funhouse, *padre*, complete with bars and restaurants, and a man named Tommy Bartlett does a spectacular water show there. They even have two Acapulco divers. That's where you belong, *padre*, in Chicago."

Father Palomo rose. "Yes, I should be in Chicago! Tell me how to get there, Gabriel, I'll leave today." He paused. "Do you have any friends there who could help me? I have little money. Perhaps I can find a rooming house. It's not important that I don't know the language, I'll manage somehow."

Gabriel got up. "I knew you'd like my suggestion, *padre*. I know only one person who can help you—a parish priest in South Chicago, *padre* Tortas, a Spaniard. He has been there for a long time, at the *Templo de Nuestra Señora de Guadalupe*. Nobody knows Chicago better than Tortas. If he takes a liking to you, there's nothing he won't do for you. If he doesn't, you'll know it—then don't count on him for anything. He has agreed to put you up while you're in Chicago. You'll have a room and meals at the rectory. Remember this: he uses the phone like a lawyer; no one can come up with information better than he can. It's the best I can do,

1

padre Manuel."

"It's more than I could have hoped for. Tell me, Gabriel, are you . . . I mean . . . were you a priest?"

"No. I was a seminarian; I'm a telegrapher." He took a slip of paper from his pocket. "Here's *padre* Tortas' address and phone number. Call him when you get to Chicago. From the bus station. They're expecting your call. It won't make any difference if he isn't in, someone will go for you when you call." They embraced and Gabriel left.

Evaristo returned in the evening and found the priest waiting for him. When he saw his valise near the door he fell to his knees saying, "Forgive me, *padre*, I meant you no harm," and he wept inconsolably. "Rise," the priest said, "you are forgiven." And then he placed his hand on the weeping man's head saying, "God is with you always," and the man stopped weeping.

Father Palomo arrived in Chicago at ten o'clock and chose not to call at that hour. It was a hot, muggy, July night. He removed his collar and sat down on a bench, holding fast to his valise. It amazed him to see luggage left unattended. He would wait until morning to call.

His hat, his black clothes, his shabbiness, the aura of utter foreignness and calm that surrounded him drew stares. A Salvationist entered the waiting room, circled it twice and approached Father Palomo. They managed to understand one another, mostly through gestures, and the uniformed man persuaded the Mexican to spend the night in a Salvation Army bed. In the morning the priest called from the mission and spoke to Father Tortas, whose voice tightened when he heard where the caller had spent the night. An hour later Father Palomo stepped out of a car and stood in front of the *Templo de Nuestra Señora de Guadalupe* in South Chicago.

Father Juan Ginés Tortas was reading in his living room when his housekeeper entered with Father Manuel Palomo. He rose to receive him and scowled upon seeing how rumpled and worn the man's clothes were. His were new, meticulously pressed. They shook hands, Father Tortas keeping his arm extended to protect himself from any attempt at an embrace. Pointing to the withered valise, he said to his housekeeper, "Marta, take that thing upstairs to the *padre*'s room." The Spaniard was standing beside an elaborately carved chair that had a high back and massive arms. With a toss of his head he indicated a small one with a caned back. "*Padre*, bring that chair and sit here with me," he said, settling into the big chair, "I must talk to you. I'm disappointed that you didn't call me last night when you got in, and deeply distressed that you felt compelled to go begging." His Spanish pronunciation, rapid and staccato, shot the words from his mouth like pellets.

"Begging? I don't understand. It was late, *padre*. I thought it better to wait until morning. But let me assure you that I did not go begging," Father Palomo answered, his Mexican Spanish full of soft sibilants.

"The Salvation Army aids beggars, *escoria humana*, riffraff! And what is more, it is run by Protestants!" Father Tortas said, slamming his fist into his palm.

Father Palomo opened his arms and explained, "A man in uniform approached me, offered me a bed. I asked for nothing. Somehow he knew I was going to spend the night there."

"It would not take clairvoyance to know that, *padre*. One look at you, your valise, your sandals . . . better to avoid drawing attention to yourself. But that is your affair. They are Protestants, and that is what concerns me."

"They are Christians, *padre*. They did me a kindness. The world is full of beggars; it lacks charitable Christians. Anyone who aids beggars is doing God's work. I was in no danger of becoming a Protestant, I assure you."

"You are a priest and a Catholic. You were consorting with Protestants. Your indiscretion, they have ways of using it against us. If you had called, you could have avoided the compromising circumstances you got into. This is not Mexico. Here," Father Tortas said, swinging his right arm in a great horizontal arc, "we are surrounded by Protestants. Heed me, *padre*, I am twice your age. You are young."

"Young? I am thirty-three. You and I probably disagree about many things, but I have not come here to disagree with you. Let us not argue. *Padre*, you'll pardon me for saying so, but you don't seem to know what poverty is," Father Palomo said, encompassing the room with a sweep of his arms and eyes. "I dress this way because I have nothing else to wear. I need nothing else. My parishioners often go hungry. That is why I am here, *padre*, to raise money for my parish."

Father Tortas clenched his teeth. "What do you want of me?" he asked.

"I must speak to those in charge of the *Aquarama*, the ship. Do you know about it?" The Spaniard nodded. "How can I reach them?"

"A boy will show you how to get downtown on the train. That way you'll be completely independent. The man you must see has an office on Navy Pier. I do not know him but he's called Captain Harry. I'll get his address for you." Father Tortas paused and looked beyond his guest for a moment.

"What is it, *padre*?" Father Palomo asked.

"A word of caution. In some curious way there is less freedom here than in Spain or Mexico. People here are less tolerant. That is, ideas of what constitutes decorous and indecorous behavior are more rigid here. Frankly, I prefer it that way. It's a matter of breeding, you know, of education. Only the poor make a spectacle of themselves, give vent to their passions. I don't know if the people in this city will want to see you, a priest, earn money publicly. I disapprove of your plans and doubt that you can get anywhere with them. The Irish priests will be watching you. All the same, I wish you luck. You're on your own, *padre*. Under no circumstances are you to involve me or my parish in your affairs. One final matter now. About your meals. If you're going to miss them or be late for them, let Marta know. I don't want her to be kept waiting."

"I understand," Father Palomo answered, and he wondered who the Irish priests were.

Father Palomo approached *Aquarama* headquarters whispering the phrases the boy Marcos had taught him. These, an envelope with newspaper clippings, and his need were what he had to sustain him. He opened the door and entered.

A young woman looked up from the desk where she was working and smiled. "Good morning," she said, regarding him. He was small-boned and wore a black cotton jersey under a black suit. An aura of frailty and strength surrounded him, as if his lean flesh were hung on a frame of fine tubular stainless.

Her smile encouraged him. Before speaking, he removed the amber-colored hat that crowned his head. "Goo-the morrneen," he said, "I wan, pleece, espeek weeth Copteen Hahrree." He studied her face for a reaction. Her hair was a cap of soft curls above a high expanse of forehead; her eyes, bright and lively, were separated by the wide bridge of a generous nose; her mouth was restless and expressive.

"I'm sorry but he isn't in. May I help you?"

"Copteen Hahree," the man said.

She knew then that he had not understood her and she spoke to him in Spanish, "*El capitán Harry no está, señor, lo siento. En que puedo servirle?"*

"*¡Ah, señorita, habla español*! What luck!" He laughed. "You understood my English?"

"*Perfectamente*," she answered, her eyes twinkling.

"Had I known I would find you here, I would not have spent so much time mastering English," he said playfully. "Where did you learn *castellano, señorita*?"

"At the university. And in Spain for a year. I want to be a Spanish teacher."

"Commendable! You'll make a good one. You know how to set a person at ease. *Señorita*, my name is Manuel Palomo," he stated, offering his hand.

"*Mucho gusto*, mine is Marianne Deeg." They shook hands.

"I'm a priest," he added.

"Yes, of couse. You look like a priest, but I wasn't sure. You aren't wearing a collar."

"It takes more than a collar to make a priest, *señorita*," he said, suddenly serious. "Some who wear collars and call themselves priests, are not."

"I suppose so, *padre*. Some spend their lives in classrooms and call themselves teachers but are not."

"It is the way of the world, *señorita*, to say that one is what one is not. I am what I am."

She smiled at his final words, but when she searched his face for some sign of playfulness, she found none.

"*Señorita*, do you know when Captain Harry will return?"

"Before noon, *padre*. Can I help you? I'm his secretary."

"It's about the ship. I wonder if he would hire me."

"Hire you, *padre*? I don't understand."

"It's not what you think, *señorita*. I'm a diver. Look." He took the clippings from the envelope and handed them to her: pictures of his high dives and accompanying stories.

She looked at the pictures and skimmed the stories. "He

already has two Acapulco divers, *padre*."

"Our diving styles are different, *señorita*. I know Acapulco divers. You would see the difference between us at once." His tone was gently suppliant, his eyes unblinking.

"Why don't you come back at eleven-thirty, *padre*. Captain Harry will be here then."

"Does Captain Harry speak Spanish, *señorita*?"

"No, *padre*," she said, handing him the clippings.

At eleven-thirty the priest returned and Marianne Deeg rose to receive him. "Ah, you're back, *padre*. Come, meet Captain Harry. Harry, this is Father Palomo, the priest I was telling you about." The men exchanged a nod and when they shook hands Father Palomo felt the man's soft palm and fingers. Deep-chested and tanned, the man was more than six feet tall. He wore casual clothes, boat shoes, a white cap with gold braid on its black visor. When he was a fisherman, Father Palomo had seen men like him in coastal fishing villages where they had gone for supplies, their yachts anchored nearby.

"Is he a sailor, *señorita*?" the priest asked.

She held back a smile and translated.

Captain Harry shook his head vigorously and laughed. "No, tell him I'm a historian," he said. "I like books, not boats. And I'm choosy about books. But I have to be a sailor in this job. I would be teaching at a university if I could put up with grading and colleagues. I don't even know how to swim. Tell him not to judge a book by its cover."

"He doesn't have sailor's hands. Will he hire me?"

Marianne and Captain Harry spoke briefly. "He says he won't decide until he knows more about you, *padre*. How you came to be a priest, learned to dive. Persuade him, *padre*."

"He can bill me as *The Diving Priest*. That's the attraction. It catches the curiosity of people. When has he ever heard of a diving priest?"

"Ask him why he wants to dive *here*. Doesn't he know this is a circus? Tell him a Chamber board controls the hiring. I can't promise anything." Marianne explained it all.

"I'm from La Huacana," the priest said, "a town in the state of Michoacán." He looked from Marianne to Captain Harry as he spoke. "An earthquake hit us last year. We lost almost everything. Our church is in need of repairs. Even in good times life is difficult for us. My parishioners have sacrificed much to get me here. I have come to earn money. I will not disappoint him if he hires me." He drew the envelope of clippings from his pocket and held it out to Captain Harry. "These will give him an idea of what I can do, *señorita*."

Marianne translated and Captain Harry looked at he clippings. "He's right about the *Diving Priest* angle," he said. "It could make a fine human interest story if it's done the right way. Contacting the newspapers is easy. The difficult thing is to sell them on doing more than just a picture and a caption. We want full coverage in the Sunday edition. And if possible, follow-ups. But I'll need a lot of good detail for this. I want everyone in the city to know about the *Aquarama*, to know what I'm doing here. Father Palomo's story may be just what I need to capture the city's interests. I have to know about his childhood, where he's lived, how he got where he is, when he began to raise money by diving. Explain it to him carefully, Marianne." And she did.

"I am not important," the priest objected, "my parishioners are. Even my diving is unimportant by itself. It means something only with respect to them. La Huacana is important. I can tell you about it."

"Captain Harry must convince the Chamber board, *padre*. It's the only way. Remember, we already have two divers. Tell him what he needs to know."

Father Palomo declined the chair they offered him, seeming to withdraw into himself. He wanted only to dive for them; they wanted to strip him of his privacy. He would give them dives they would not forget, but behind those dives his person must remain hidden. He had come to perform, not to confess, and they were asking him for a general confession. He needed money and he had told them why. And because of that need he would have to give it to them. There was no way out.

They sat down and he stood facing them, lean, pensive, silent, his hands clasped at his chest. He told them a spare story of his widowed mother, who raised four small sons in poverty in the coastal town where she had taken them, where he learned to fish and where his obsession with pelicans was born; of leaving home at the age of twelve and living in villages on the Pacific coast where he fished and learned to dive; of the death of his mother and brother, and of the guilt and remorse that led him, with the help of a priest, to the seminary.

They questioned him about details. He answered them laconically, evading their queries whenever he could, resisting their attempts to make him reveal himself and instead making them feel the keen need of his flock. He brought his story to an end saying, "That's how I learned to dive and that's how I became a priest. I have dived for my parishioners whenever I could. But there are few places and occasions to dive in Mexico. In Acapulco you must keep at it constantly, for those waters are treacherous." He threw his hands up and added, "There is no money in Mexico for the poor or the priests of the poor. That is why I dive. *Señorita*, tell Captain Harry it isn't difficult to dive from great heights, it's a matter of getting used to it. High divers attract attention because heights terrify and fascinate people. Do you know what is difficult and important? The way you breathe, the way you think of what you are doing and want to do, the way you give yourself

1

to the dive. I try to imagine that I'm a pelican." His eyes went back and forth from Marianne to her boss.

Captain Harry got up from his chair and stood before the priest, as if he were measuring him, or measuring himself against him. Then he said, "I'll help you, Father. Tell him, Marianne, I'll do everything I can to help him."

"You won't regret it," Father Palomo responded. And in a rush of enthusiasm he embraced the big man, who stiffened with confusion and shifted from one foot to the other.

In the early morning Father Palomo spoke to Father Tortas. "*Padre*, I've come to say good-bye. Captain Harry wants me near the *Aquarama*. You helped me immensely, thank you."

"Have things worked out for you?"

"Not yet, but I am hopeful. I regret not having said a single Mass for you, *padre*. I wanted to help. Perhaps I can when I'm more settled."

"That won't be necessary, *padre*. My Mass schedule is inflexible, I set it up each month. I abhor any departure from discipline. Visiting priests have caused me problems in the past. My flock does not graze in open pastures. My duty is to protect my sheep and I do it whether they like it or not."

"As you wish, *padre*. Should you ever visit La Huacana, my very humble home would be yours, and I, your servant."

"I never will, *padre*. Life here is difficult enough. I came here when I was younger than you, full of hope and ambition, and I'm still here, in the very same place. I look for simplicity in life. It is a principle everyone should follow. What is the name of the church where you will be?"

"I will be downtown, *padre*. Captain Harry has taken a room for me at the YMCA. Do you know it?"

"The YMCA? It is a hive for Protestant bees! Don't you ask questions when you find yourself in strange places so that you'll know who your friends and enemies are? You've been misled! What do you plan to do about it, *padre*?"

"To stay at the YMCA! Captain Harry is my friend; he wants to help me find a way to raise money for my flock. That's why I'm here, *padre*, to earn money! To fulfill my responsibility! He has offered to pay for my room and meals and I have accepted his offer. He says I must be near the ship, and I will, even if I have to stay in Hell! Can you do more for me than this Captain Harry? Give me better advice?"

"Go! Go quickly!" the Spaniard threatened, "before I lose my patience with you. You skip from one country to another doing as you please without regard for anyone but yourself. And you call yourself a priest!"

"Marianne, do you know the Right Reverend Monsignor Edmond Byrne at the Chancery Office?" Captain Harry asked her when she arrived.

The name triggered recollections. After graduation from Rosary College in 1951, she had taken a job at Loyola's Lewis Towers as secretary to the Director of Public Relations. Through 1953 she had orchestrated the Cardinal's Dinner and each November the event had culminated in glittering success. At two hundred and fifty dollars a plate, it was the most important Catholic social occasion of the year. It was held at the Conrad Hilton, formerly the Stevens, and the wealthiest Catholics from the city and suburbs were always in attendance, as were the most important prelates. She had met Cardinal Stritch, knew well his most trusted Lieutenant, Monsignor James Hardiman, and had dealt with the priests at the Chancery Office. "Of course I do," she answered. "I met him when I worked at Lewis Towers. I used to see him about the Cardinal's Dinner. He's the Archdiocesan Chancellor. Why do you ask?"

"He has agreed to see Father Palomo at ten-thirty this morning. They need a translator. Go with him."

"See Father Palomo for what, Harry?"

"Come on, Marianne, we can't hire Father Palomo without going through official channels. This thing's too public. The Archdiocese would hit the ceiling. I thought you understood."

"What a jerk! Of course! I should have, but I've thought only of Father Palomo's need."

"You're supposed to know about public relations, that's why I hired you." He winked. "And you put together the Cardinal's Dinner?" he asked teasingly. "Look," he went on, serious now, "Father Palomo's joining us will be a matter of great concern to the Archdiocese. He'll have to get permission to dive and we need it to bill him as *The Diving Priest*. I was hired to generate good will, and the last thing I need is a public quarrel with the city's ranking Catholic Prelates." He paused. "What about this Byrne, what's he like?"

She thought for a moment then said, "He tends to be impersonal and is a stickler for rules and formality, but he's fair, I'm sure of it. He was always pleasant. He used to joke about a Chancellor's Dinner, said it would let the faithful know that he, not the Cardinal, was the expert in canon law. The other priests all seemed to like him."

"Did you know him well?"

"I felt I did, but my contact with him was limited. I could always reach him, even on short notice."

"Well, this isn't the Cardinal's Dinner we're working on, so if you have any influence anywhere, use it."

At ten o'clock, walking at an easy pace, they left for the Chancery Office on Wabash, just east of Holy Name Cathedral. It was Thursday. Along the Magnificent Mile they crossed Michigan Avenue.

Father Palomo noticed a jauntiness in Marianne's stride and turned to look at her. She was blooming with vitality in her full-skirted yellow dress, her radiance equal to the sun's. He was aware now that his black clothes were a blot on the sea of bright colors around him, but he went forward effortlessly on small feet that seemed not to touch the ground. Suddenly he thought of his parishioners and the attendant pang made him speak. "This avenue, *señorita*, it reminds me of El Paseo de la Reforma in Mexico City. But where are the poor? The vendors of lottery tickets? The children who sell newspapers and gum? Have you no poor here?"

She answered him haltingly, "I don't know, *padre* . . . for some reason . . . the poor never come to this part of the city." They walked on in silence and then she spoke again, "I have never been to Mexico City, *padre*. That *paseo* you mentioned, it must be very beautiful."

"Yes, it is, very. I'm sure you would like it."

Marianne felt the past wash over her as she and Father Palomo approached the Chancery. She was anticipating their meeting— they would have a pleasant conversation with Monsignor Byrne and he would grant the permission they needed. Then she and Captain Harry and Father Palomo would sail on with their plans for the latter's debut.

They went from the brilliance of the street into the Chancery and found themselves in darkness—a poorly lit interior panelled with wood and appointed with deeply carved furniture that conjured up power and tradition. Father Palomo's shoulders sagged. A secretary told them to be seated.

They were kept waiting until eleven-thirty when a voice ordered, "Send them up now." Wearing a beautifully tailored cassock with red piping and a red sash at the waist, the Right

Reverend Monsignor Edmond Byrne received them at the top of the stairs. "Is this the priest who wants to dive?" he asked in a manner that left no room for introductions. Marianne realized that he did not recognize her. He looked at his watch and spoke before she could answer, "I have a luncheon engagement at noon and can't be late, so we don't have much time. Who is he? Where is he from? And why in God's name would he want to make a spectacle of himself at that circus on Navy Pier? Ask him," he ordered, glaring at the man from head to sandals and bringing his eyes to rest on the straw hat in Father Palomo's hands.

They were standing in the narrow hallway to one side of the stairs and it was clear that Monsignor Byrne had no intention of taking them into his office. Marianne began to explain, "He's from a small . . . "

"Let him tell me!" the Chancellor screamed. "You translate, nothing more!" The pink flesh under his chin quivered.

"Padre, he wants to know who you are, where you're from, why you want to dive," Marianne said, her voice unsteady.

Father Palomo put his hat down on a chair, approached the Chancellor and stood before him, his arms reaching just below his belt buckle, hands crossed at the wrists as if they were tied. He had understood the man's tone perfectly. "Tell him I'm the priest of a poor parish in Mexico. An earthquake did a lot of damage in my village—to our church, to the houses of my parishioners, who lost many things. I've come to raise money to help them." Marianne translated.

"Tell him he has no business being here. His is a problem for the Mexican Hierarchy, not for us. If it were serious we would have heard about it. What's more, he cannot swoop down on us unannounced, unsponsored. I've had to cancel an appointment with one of my own priests to see him. His superiors should have called to ask for permission for him to come. What a mess we'd be in if everybody did things like him! His problems belong in Mexico City. Can't he dive in Mexico?"

"Tell him, *señorita*, that there are no solutions for my problems in Mexico City. That's why I've come here." He nodded vigorously and added, "Yes, I can dive in Mexico, but there are few opportunities. I do high dives that can be dangerous." He took the envelope of clippings from his pocket and held it out to the Chancellor. "These will help him understand."

Monsignor Byrne grimaced as he flipped through the clippings. "My God, he missed his calling, he's a circus performer, not a priest! No wonder he fell in with that *Aquarama* crowd. Ask him if he's a real priest." He turned on Father Palomo in anger and shouted, "Are you ordained?"

"Yes, I'm an ordained priest. I worry about the least of my parishioners. He must give me permission to dive. In Mexico I don't have to ask for permission."

"I don't care what he does in Mexico. That's his business, theirs. But what he does in the Chicago diocese is mine. No! He cannot dive here! In Chicago we believe that it's beneath the dignity of the Church to place a priest on exhibition. Tell him!"

Father Palomo threw his arms open and addressed the Chancellor directly. Marianne's voice wavered, "Please let me dive. My parishioners, what will they do?" Then he backed away from the Chancellor. "I cannot accept your decision. Is there anyone else I can talk to?"

"Do you know who I am?" the Chancellor screeched. "Mine is the final word in this matter. Disobey me and you will regret it, I warn you. You are insubordinate, and an insubordinate priest is no priest at all. You are not a priest!"

Captain Harry was waiting when they returned. One look told him the worst had happened. Father Palomo, abstracted, went to the window. Marianne's words struggled against the silence, "He was ugly . . . to the two of us . . . and I was completely unprepared for it . . . that side of the Church . . . I'd never seen it. My God, he was brutal with Father Palomo."

"What happened?"

"It all seemed so easy to me . . . He didn't give us a chance, wouldn't listen to anything. He didn't even recognize me . . . I was so naive, Harry . . . so stupid!"

Captain Harry went to the window. He placed a hand on the priest's shoulder; the priest did not move. "I'm sorry, Father," he apologized, "I really wanted to help you. It's out of my hands now. They've made it impossible for me, for you."

The priest turned to look at the big man. "Captain Harry," he said, "we are what we are. Your intention has not been lost. In God's eyes you have helped me. Our mistake was in asking for permission. I shall not do that again. Tomorrow I must leave. My parishioners need me. You and Marianne have done much for me and I have caused Monsignor Byrne to think of you as unscrupulous circus masters. I won't forget you." He was standing between them. "If only I had something to give you, as a mark of my gratitude." He fell silent, but immediately afterwards said, "In the morning, early, before others arrive, I'll dive for you. It's all I have to give. Will you accept it?"

Without hesitation, Marianne said, "*Sí, padre.*"

It was cool, the morning pale and limpid, the pier silent and abandoned when they reached the *Aquarama* and went on board. Captain Harry guided the priest to a small washroom and waited outside. Haggard and shivering, Father Palomo appeared shortly thereafter wearing only a swimsuit. On bare feet he followed the other man unsteadily, swaying as if he carried a great weight. Captain Harry led him to the narrow ladder that reached into the sky alongside the specially constructed mast that ended in a tiny platform. Father Palomo put his hands on a rung, tipped his head back and lifted his eyes. Visibly upset, he turned his eyes on the man and woman beside him.

"Father," Captain Harry said, "you don't have to do it, we understand. Tell him, Marianne."

"You don't understand," he said, "I must do it." And he started up the ladder, making the long ascent slowly and did not rest until he was standing on the platform.

In the east the sun had shattered the horizon and mounted rapidly, crimsoning the lake as Father Palomo prepared to dive. He pushed off with his feet, launching himself forward, his arms extended at his sides like wings, palms open, and then the wind seemed to catch and lift him and for a moment the two witnesses thought he would be suspended there forever. As he began to fall, he drew his head back sharply, pelican-like, and struggling against the world's forces, arched his spine so deeply that his body seemed to break. Abruptly his struggle ended. Somehow he slowed his fall, and they lost all sense of time as they watched him miraculously right his body ninety degrees until his feet were under him at the extremity of the line, traced against the sky, that ran straight down from his head and crossed perpendicularly the span of his open arms. As if glimpsing eternity, they saw him hang there for an endless moment, his fall arrested.

The descent came swiftly, and then his feet struck the crimson waters below and, as it disappeared, his body sent an enormous plume fanning across the sky, eclipsing the morning sun. They lost sight of him in the lake's shimmering agitation, took alarm when it calmed and he did not appear. Then they saw him at a great depth, rising through the still waters, and when he rent the surface, his face flushed, radiant, they cried out.